Praise for *Between the Lines*

"[*Between the Lines*] is a journey to sexual fulfillment bristling with smart, intense dialogue between two characters who are definitely more than women-loving-women romance novel stereotypes."—Richard Labonte, Book Marks

"*Between The Lines* is an excellent read for that lazy, sensual weekend where you need a little romance in your heart, a little laughter in your soul, and a good read for that moment of escape. The characters in this book are eccentric and comedic… There're fun, sexy, romantic, and heartfelt moments embedded into the pages as the story unfolds."—*Kissed by Venus*

By the Author

Between the Lines

Loving Liz

Coming Attractions: Author's Edition

COMING

ATTRACTIONS
AUTHOR'S EDITION

by

Bobbi Marolt

2012

COMING ATTRACTIONS: AUTHOR'S EDITION
© 1997, 2012 By Bobbi Marolt. All Rights Reserved.

ISBN 13: 978-1-60282-732-5

This Trade Paperback Original Is Published By
Bold Strokes Books, Inc.
P.O. Box 249
Valley Falls, NY 12185

Printed in August 2012

CREDITS
EDITOR: CINDY CRESAP
PRODUCTION DESIGN: STACIA SEAMAN
COVER DESIGN BY SHERI (GRAPHICARTIST2020@HOTMAIL.COM)

Acknowledgments

Lynn, who horsewhipped me into getting this work completed.

Melissa, who I know is grinning (knock it off) after my protestations of a rewrite.

Pam Sloss and Terri Baker for requesting a new release.

Sheri, for another perfect cover.

Thanks, y'all.

To the performing arts and artists that move me.

FROM THE AUTHOR'S MESSY DESK:

In 1997, *Coming Attractions* was first published. Through the years, and for many reasons, I'd look at the book and wish I had another crack at editing. A few (less than ten) words and phrases were inserted that I'd never have any characters say. I also found issues with grammar, punctuation, repetition, exclamation points, and various whatnot that made me cringe, and all were my fault. If I only had another chance…

My wish upon a star was granted. Radclyffe forwarded an e-mail from a reader who wanted to see the story reprinted by Bold Strokes. Did I want to do an author's edition? Rad asked. Hell, yeah!

Be careful of your wishes.

From the first to the final page, the newer edition became a nightmare for me. There was rarely a sentence that my editor, Cindy Cresap, would have been happy with. To the aforementioned problems, add poorly placed modifiers, a sudden and brief POV change, dangling modifiers…the list goes on. I firmly believe if she read the original publication, she'd exhibit the proverbial run and scream into the night. She might have even slapped me, just because. I don't know.

I ignored the work and tried to pretend that my contract with BSB didn't exist. That was sure to catch up with me, and when it did, I had about five weeks to complete the project. Eventually, I was forced to buy another month from Cindy, because I hadn't edited another word beyond Chapter Two (you may now take a breath). Granted the month, I worked the words into a more acceptable state (I didn't edit the brief POV change) and sent a new draft—a week late.

Jump to edits. Not so bad after her critical eyes. Naturally, she snagged me on the different point of view that I'd left. Rewriting and relocating 4,000 words was tough, but I got through it. I must admit that the story reads better.

What readers will now find is a refined edition and one that I feel much better about presenting. There is a completely new chapter (taken from the original 90,000 words) that adds dimension to Helen. A second love scene has been extended, and many scenes have been improved upon. The story, of course, remains the same.

Personal notes:

My working title of *Coming Attractions* was *Etude* (italics intended). It's the title I still prefer.

The original manuscript was 90,000 words. The original published manuscript was 47,000 words. The Bold Strokes Books Author's Edition is approximately 53,000 words.

The story still makes me tearful after all these years.

I must have a thing for the House of Tudor, as I've mentioned them in two novels.

The two Chopin pieces—"Polonaise No. 3 in A, Op. 40 No.1, Military," and "Etude Op. 10, No.3 in E Tristesse"—are my favorites, preferably played by Vladimir Ashkenazy.

Chapter Five is my pet. I thoroughly enjoyed writing Helen's obsessive nature.

Thanks for reading.

—b

CHAPTER ONE

Newspaper columnist Helen Townsend leaned back into her leather chair, held the phone away from her ear, and studied the buildings outside her office window. Steel and concrete were more interesting than the chastising she received from another irate reader. Today, her column defended abortion rights.

Helen half listened to the woman's song and dance, which included God, murder, and souls damned forever. Seemingly, the speech was Helen's private Muzak, cleverly disguised as the phone company. Enough was enough.

While the woman squawked, Helen cradled the handset on her lap. She rolled her shoulders and then straightened the clutter of notes, pencils, and stray floppy disks on her desk. Her computer clock read five twenty, and she turned off the monitor. For the night, she was officially off the company payroll, and it was time to go home. She looked at the phone receiver briefly, put it closer to her face, and then politely blew her caller out of the water.

"I understand your position," she said and kicked off her high heels. "If you're so dead set against abortion, then don't have one. It's my opinion that others deserve a choice." She reached under her desk and pulled on her sneakers.

A loud crash on the other end of the line signaled the

conversation had ended. Helen shook her head and replaced the receiver. She would have appreciated one positive response. Where were her advocates? Amid the entirely negative reactions, a simple, "Hey, Helen, good column," would have been sufficient. She struggled with putting her jacket on and then flipped her hair from under the collar. "Hell, then I wouldn't have anything to bitch about."

Hers was just another day at the office and Helen liked her profession. No, she loved having the good, the bad, and the ugly of New York at her fingertips and then writing about them. She would never please everyone, but the job was fun and Sam, her editor, trusted her judgment.

❖

Outside the building, the weather was unseasonable and she closed her eyes to a sudden burst of chilled air. She shivered and turned her collar up. That wind was much too cold for the beginning of October. With winter not far behind, she knew time neared for steady workouts.

"Women don't sweat, they glisten." She laughed to herself.

"Helen Townsend?" a woman called from behind her.

Helen cringed, expecting another save-the-world-before-we-all-go-to-hell-mother-of-five-who-will-not-tolerate-abortions-or-any-person-connected-with-them. She spun around and shot a defensive look toward the woman.

"Yes, I'm Helen, but if you want to blast me about today's column, feel free to call my office tomorrow. Right now, all I'm interested in is a hot bath and a cheeseburger."

The woman stepped back, studied Helen's face, and gave a slight laugh. "Judging from your defensiveness, I assume you've had quite a column today." She glanced over Helen's shoulder. "I wanted to say that I took particular interest in your black sheep column a few weeks ago."

When she looked back at Helen, the intruder's eyes quickly drew Helen into them. Embarrassed, Helen stammered, "I have to apologize. I've been damned to hell so much today that—"

"Apology accepted."

She was close in age to Helen, but stood a good four inches shorter than Helen's five feet six inches. Straight, dark brown hair cascaded past her shoulders, and Helen wondered where it ended. A wisp of bangs hung over her forehead; her eyebrows lay erratic, and Helen was enticed to reach over to smooth them, but she didn't. She actually liked the look. The woman smiled easily with her naturally pink mouth.

Thick, dark lashes and brilliant emeralds of near-perfect clarity gripped Helen. It was a deliberate possession and she wanted to run but felt an impulse, a distinct need, to pull the woman tightly to her and seal her mouth around her soft lips. Flustered with immediate want, she was certain her blush gave her away.

"Be careful," the woman said with obvious amusement. "Between your look and your black sheep column, you're revealing a great deal about yourself. Good-bye, Ms. Townsend, and I hope you have an enjoyable evening." She turned and walked away.

A weakening rush overcame Helen when she noticed the woman's hair fell nearly to the middle of her back. Come back! Stop! Wait! Her mind raced. Careful. Black sheep. Revealing. She needed to have the statement deciphered. Helen quickly wove her way through pedestrians and the smell of street vendors' hot dogs, until she reached the woman.

"What did you mean by that?" Helen reached out, carefully grabbed the woman's arm, and kept pace with her.

Composed, the woman turned her head toward Helen and

smiled. "I meant, have a nice evening, and I hope you'll get that cheeseburger."

"No, what do you mean about revealing myself?" Helen spoke directly to the captivating eyes. She wanted to dive into them and swim around to search for the intended answer.

"I mean your look could have easily been mistaken for a pass."

Helen was too flustered to see the pedestrian who bumped into her and shoved her helplessly into the steadying hands of the woman. Blaring horns, the stench of exhaust, the intrusive bump of pedestrians—all of New York disappeared. Face-to-face, only they remained, and their lips were inches apart. A strong gust of wind blew the woman's hair, enough that it grazed Helen's cheek. The light scent of lily of the valley tantalized Helen. Perfume or shampoo, it didn't matter. Wondrous eyes consumed Helen. Torrents of heat tore through her and her heartbeat quickened into cannon fire. Those feelings, which at one time fascinated her, now frightened her. She stepped back and delivered a pathetic clearing of her throat.

"It wasn't anything like that," she said. "You have lovely eyes, and I didn't mean to offend you."

"I'm not offended. I'm flattered, and especially coming from a woman of your standing." The woman's lips parted and she took in a quick breath of air. Helen expected her to say more but instead heard an unsatisfying conclusion. "Good night, Ms. Townsend." She turned away and proceeded up Fifth Avenue.

Helen was still standing? How could that be possible when she hadn't even breathed in two minutes?

"Wait!" She sounded desperate, but she couldn't let the woman go. "Do you have a name?"

"Yes," she answered over her shoulder and continued her walk.

"Yes?" Helen repeated and scowled. "That's a lovely name, smart-ass." As her facial muscles relaxed, she corrected herself, and the woman fully disappeared into the crowd. "She's a lovely smart-ass."

Helen turned around and headed south. She had no time for games and tried to write off the encounter as just another New York minute, but she couldn't disregard the immediacy of her desire. Don't go there. Chasing turns to caring turns to loving turns to leaving. Comfort and satisfaction came from her work, and she was now used to the single life. That was all she needed.

❖

She searched her home computer files for the black sheep column and finished a take-out burger while she waited for the soft hum of the printer to stop.

Helen pulled the page from the tray and went into her bedroom. She stripped herself of confining office clothes and slipped into a fine black satin robe. Too cold. She tore it off and threw it to the chair. She then grabbed the vanilla terry cloth robe, pulled the cuddly garment around her, and stretched belly first onto the bed. She grabbed the paper from the nightstand and scanned the printed page, which she mumbled aloud.

"…children who stray from the supposed normalcy of family life…moved away…never married…brother is attorney…black sheep receive questions from intolerant families…no clear answers…fear of being ostracized. What if a father asks his thirty-six-year-old daughter why she hasn't married? How can she tell him of her preference for women when his attitude is that all homosexuals should be shot?"

Helen put the page down and propped herself on one elbow. "I think Ms. Green Eyes is a dyke."

She looked back at the paper on the bed. Written two months ago, that column was her expression of restlessness, her way of giving voice to her own anger for allowing herself to remain in the closet. It hadn't been her coming out column, though. She wasn't ready then. Now she was ready and expected to do it with both barrels smoking. What she really wanted to say in the black sheep column, and what she fervently wanted to say now, was, "News flash: I'm a dyke. Print that baby on the front page and don't get the name wrong. It's Helen, and why not capitalize that L?" She sighed. "Yeah, right. An active lesbian, no, but I still deserve my rights."

Although her desire was based entirely on women, men weren't absent in her life. There was, for instance, Tom Winsloe, whom she affectionately called Tucson, after his hometown. He was a rugged, handsome man and to see him you wouldn't know he was, in his own words, "just another fag." Holding membership within New York's finest press corps, they attended social functions together. An occasional photograph of the two of them hand in hand kept the nosy at bay.

Helen had met Chelsea through Tucson. "She's the perfect woman for you," he said. "She's intelligent, artistic, and the funniest woman this side of the Mississippi."

"Absolutely not," she said to his suggestion for a blind date, and leaned back against the rail of the ferry that transported them from Ellis Island.

"You have to trust me, Helen."

"Trust you? Your last perfect woman wouldn't keep her hands off of me." She pointed to the imposing Statue of Liberty behind him. "I'd have felt safer with someone green."

"PMS. Loss of hormone control," he said.

Helen was ready to toss him overboard. "I beg your pardon. That Amazon had a tattoo of a serpent on her thigh."

She shook her head vigorously at the memory of wrestling away from the arms of the snake woman. "Keep your perfect date away from me."

When he had shown her a photo of a woman with soft, curly blond hair, Helen found her adorable. She happily gave in to an introduction, and Tucson found redemption. Neither Helen nor Chelsea had experienced such a loving and full relationship before they'd met. After three years together, they were ready for the long haul when the love of Helen's life heard a medical diagnosis that held no promises of happily ever after.

Helen remembered Chelsea's final months.

❖

"Pancreatic cancer," Dr. Teresa Santos said. "Chelsea, I want you to see an oncologist at Sloan-Kettering Cancer Center."

A shock wave ripped through Helen. She gripped Chelsea's hand and their eyes met. Chelsea was strong, but she remained quiet. Helen saw tremors on her lip, tears she tried to hold back, and the urgency in her eyes that pleaded for help.

Helen's throat choked her words. "Cancer is curable," she said. "We'll fight it and you'll beat it." Chelsea would not die. Helen wouldn't allow it. She turned to the doctor. "There's therapy, right? Radiation? Chemo?"

Helen saw no mercy in Dr. Santos's eyes. What was wrong with her? The physician's job was to ensure the life of the woman Helen loved. Find a pill, damn it. Create a miracle. Bombard Chelsea with enough radiation to make Marie Curie stand up from her grave and applaud. Dear God, don't take Chelsea's life.

Dr. Santos laced her fingers together; the tips of her index fingers rested on her lips, thumbs supported her chin. This is the church and this is the steeple. An unheard prayer to the gods of medicine? She sat back and rested her hands on the arms of her chair. She looked at Helen and then at Chelsea.

"Chelsea, I won't mislead you."

Abruptly, Helen leaned forward. "Mislead her how?"

Chelsea pulled her back in the seat. "Let her finish," she said quietly.

"Dr. Hellman—the oncologist—can provide therapy, but the disease isn't one we've treated with much success."

"What the hell is that supposed to mean?" Helen shouted, ready to whisk Chelsea out of the office. It wasn't Dr. Santos's job to impose a death sentence.

Chelsea remained firm. "Let her finish. I have to hear the bottom line."

Dr. Santos gave Chelsea a year. Reality proved her overoptimistic.

Shove a stick of butter in a microwave oven for a minute. Watch while an unseen aggressor transforms the solid to liquid. Witness how quickly the molecules of fat speed up, scatter, and soon lie unrecognizable. You jam your finger on the stop button, but it doesn't work. You yank the handle, but the door won't give. You pound the glass, slam the top, rip the plug from the wall, but you've lost control and the process continues relentlessly.

Helen could only watch while the disease devoured Chelsea. A beautiful, vital woman melted into sunken features, the ravages of a starved body. Food, fluid, chemicals—none was an ally. There were no allies. Useless radiation treatments weakened her. Vomiting from chemicals had increased pain, drained life, and she struggled to remain alive.

"I want to go home," she said from her hospital bed. "I don't want to die here."

One night, during the fifth month after the diagnosis, Chelsea's previous hours were her most painful yet, and Helen was ready with morphine when asked for the medication.

"Hey, Townsend," Chelsea whispered.

Helen snapped awake and was angry for having fallen asleep in her chair. She moved to Chelsea's side. "I'm here, sweetheart."

"Help me up."

Helen avoided the IV tubing that fed the disintegrating body before her. Chelsea barely weighed eighty pounds and her ribs felt ready to puncture her thin skin. Helen lifted carefully and held gently.

"What do you need?" she whispered while Chelsea, the love of her life, lay dying in her arms.

"You." She groaned. "I love you."

Helen bit her lip. The lump in her throat stole her voice and she swallowed hard. "Yes, I know," she wanted to say. "And I love you too and I don't want you to hurt anymore and please get better so I can say I love you for fifty more years." Helen's body shook. None of those words would come and none of those things would happen. She could only nod.

Somewhere between Helen's nod and a kiss to Chelsea's forehead, Chelsea died in Helen's embrace.

❖

Helen placed the black sheep printout on her dresser and then blew her nose. Her mirrored reflection showed puffy eyes. She picked up the silver-framed photograph of Chelsea and herself, the one taken on their second anniversary. It was three years since her death and Helen had remained alone.

Startled by the ringing telephone, she let the machine answer.

"You home, Blondie? Pick up."

She reached for the bedroom extension when she heard the voice of her closest friend, Stacey. "To what do I owe this honor?"

"You're supposed to be here tonight. Remember?"

"Oh. The club. I'm sorry, Stacey. I completely forgot about your party." She wiped her eyes and sniffed softly.

"You sound stuffy. Are you all right?"

"Allergies. I can't go out feeling this way." A feeble response. Stacey knew Helen had no allergies.

"You're crying again. I wish you'd stop wallowing in the past and make a new life for yourself. Put on your Sunday best and come over. A friend is giving a private recital and I want you to meet her."

She considered the offer, but tonight would be another night alone with her memories. "No, I won't let go of Chelsea." To appease Stacey, she quickly redirected the conversation. "I met a woman today."

"That's encouraging. Maybe I know her."

Helen laughed about her absurd encounter. "I never got her name, but she had incredible eyes."

"Really?" she asked and listened until Helen completed her tale. "She sounds yummy. How will you find her?"

"I haven't thought about it. I don't necessarily want to find her."

"Maybe you should think about it, or maybe she'll find you again." Helen had no response. "Are you sure you don't want to come over? If your mystery woman is a dyke, she might show up."

"Another time. I promise. Good night, Stacey."

❖

She eased into a hot bath, and her chilled body immediately sucked in the warmth. Stacey didn't understand that the love Helen felt for Chelsea hadn't stopped with her death. She'd been left behind to awaken alone, to work countless hours, and to sit in the dark and cry. Helen's memories of Chelsea haunted her every day: her art that hung on Helen's walls, her laughter that still rang in Helen's ears, her incredible need for munching pecans, and her love for a snowy day. Her tenderness. Helen held blatantly on to those memories.

And yet, as if death could ever offer fairness, Helen felt cheated. There were too many destroyed plans. Among them, their desire to have a child that Chelsea would carry, and a possible move to Scarsdale. Chelsea had promised to love Helen forever. "…from this day forward…" The words betrayed Helen, but how could Chelsea have known? "…until death…"

She cried. "You never said good-bye or go to hell."

Helen was selfish with her memories, and she thrived on them. Every time she closed her eyes, Chelsea was there, coaxing her into her arms. Helen felt Chelsea's love even after her death. She followed Helen to bed, sometimes to the bath. Those memories, those moments, they were all Helen had.

She leaned back in the tub and a wave of warm water splashed over her breasts. She closed her eyes. Chelsea smiled and her blue eyes sparkled. "Let me love you," they said to Helen. She raised her knees, and opened her legs against the cold ceramic. Helen dipped her hand into the hot water and traced the inside of her thighs.

"Chelsea." Her breaths were ragged splinters of sound.

Slowly, she teased herself with a zigzag pattern and brushed fine, floating hair. Chelsea's blue eyes suddenly flashed emerald. Helen stopped. She opened her eyes, confused by the intrusion. She caught her breath.

She closed her eyes again. Chelsea reached. The tingling down the back of Helen's legs strengthened. "Chelsea. I love you." Emerald eyes twinkled back. No!

In her mind, Helen was hurtled back to Fifth Avenue, to captive eyes, to arms that held her securely. She groaned and stroked the tiniest bit of muscle that took control.

"Do you have a name?" the muscle whispered.

"Yes," she whimpered and stroked it.

It yelled to her. "Do you have a name?"

"Yes," she groaned and stroked it.

It screamed, "Do you have a name?"

Helen gripped the tub with one hand. Water sloshed over the side of the bathtub while she led into a quick and powerful release.

Through tear-soaked eyes, she looked down to the wet, tiled floor. Left shaken, she leaned back and closed her eyes. Helen conjured Chelsea's image. Her mind struggled to sharpen the hazy shadows of curly hair that framed Chelsea's face. The quick flash of her image snapped on and then went dark until a newer picture emerged, snowy and then clear. Blue eyes shone brightly in the foreground.

"I'm sorry, Chels," Helen sobbed. "It's you I still want." The image faded. "Don't leave me," she pleaded, but the imagined eyes sharpened to deepest green.

Helen touched the tiniest bit of muscle. Her body twitched.

"Do you have a name?" the muscle asked.

"Yes," she whispered.

CHAPTER TWO

S am Baker was editor of the *New York News* and had known Helen for fifteen years. She was fresh out of college when she waved her master's degree in journalism under his nose and, having found her enthusiasm soldieresque, he allowed her the status of cub reporter. Not a glamorous post, but it was a beginning.

For starters, Sam tossed Helen a weekly opinion column and turned her loose on the streets. From Staten Island to Long Island, she fired questions to the public on capital punishment, religion in schools, and even the change in the New York skyline since the addition of the Twin Towers. New Yorkers grew to like Helen. She earned their respect and soon they came to her with topics to sharpen her skills.

A mother from Brooklyn had let her in on what she thought to be a local daycare swindle. Helen submitted an idea to Sam. She wanted to go undercover as an employee, but he wanted her to snoop around with her press badge in full view.

"We aren't cops," he said flatly.

Helen groaned, obliged, and with annoying persistence, blew the lid off a major money-laundering ring. The criminals got the slammer, the police got the glory, and Helen got a three-days-a-week featured column, along with Sam's respect. His cub was a bear.

However, the bear soon collapsed with the proper ammunition.

Helen was in her sixth year at the paper when she lost both parents in an automobile accident. Her father was driving, suffered cardiac arrest, and slammed into a tree. His death was instantaneous, but her mother, his only passenger, died a day later of head injuries.

Sam and Stacey seldom left Helen's side during the week that followed. Helen, purveyor of words, internalized her grief while Sam and Stacey led her through the horrible process of burial arrangements and then the funerals. It wasn't denial of death she experienced, but complete shock. Sam kept her afloat and only once, aside from an occasional "yes" or "no," had she commented on what should be.

"I want my mother dressed in blue."

Stacey saw to her request and nobody saw Helen place a pink hair ribbon into her father's hand. That piece of satin compelled Helen to fulfill his desire. She would write the book of his World War II experience that he had obsessed over.

Helen didn't cry until three days after their burial.

"Can we go out on your boat?" she asked Sam.

"Sure. Want to give Stacey a call?"

"No. Just us."

❖

Sam steered the forty-foot vessel around Long Island and pointed out an occasional landmark. Helen sat quietly and held no interest in his stories. Her thoughts were with her parents as she stared at the worn black-and-white photo that she held. Her mother was a young, lovely bride whose wedding dress was probably borrowed, as times were hard on the wallet. Her father stood proud in his government-issued uniform. They were married one week before he shipped out to Germany.

She could have sat there, gone through her childhood, her love for them and his heroic contribution during the liberation of the death camps, but that would have to come later. The boat ride held a different purpose.

As they neared Port Jefferson, Helen signaled for Sam to stop. She walked to the stern of the fishing cruiser and said a silent prayer for her parents. After a deep breath, she forced a guttural and increasingly loud scream, until she heard the echo throughout the Sound. Sam ran to her and Helen fell into his arms.

"It's okay, honey. Let it out," he said while she bawled and shook against his shoulder.

❖

Over the following years, Sam loved her like a daughter, came to know her better than she understood, and had enough wisdom to stay out of her personal life, until today.

Sam summoned her, and not too pleasantly, into his office. "Townsend! Get in here. Please," he added, in a gentler tone.

Townsend? Sam never called her by her last name unless he was annoyed. Helen looked around his doorway and into his office.

"Yeah?"

"Sit down." He looked at the paper in his hand and then at her. "On Monday you wrote a great column on choice, and Wednesday was pretty good with overpaid athletes." He held an unlit cigar to his mouth, rubbed it under his nose, and then tapped it like a pencil on his desktop. "But what the hell is this piece about? Explain your invisible people."

"I thought I was quite clear."

"Call me stupid." He clasped his hands behind his head and waited for her answer.

"There's an invisible world of closeted lesbians and gay men in our society," she explained. "Because they don't fit the gay stereotype, they're treated with respect. Invisible gays might work on this paper. We wouldn't have the slightest clue that Julie in accounting is sleeping with Rhonda in Human Resources."

Sam's furry white eyebrows shot to their limit. "Julie and Rhonda are sleeping together?"

"That's not what I'm saying and it's exactly what I'm saying. They look straight, but that's merely an assumption."

"I don't understand."

"The column is straightforward, and no pun intended. Equal treatment. Butches and queens should have the same rights and respect as the invisible homosexuals."

With a grunt, Sam hoisted himself from his chair and walked to the window. He scanned the street below. "Be careful," he said to the glass and walked back to his desk.

"Of what?"

"This." He drummed his fingers against Helen's Friday column.

Helen rolled her eyes. "I know I'll get a billion calls. I'm ready for them."

"No. I'm concerned about you." He sat down again. "This, and your black sheep column, tell your story."

The black sheep bullshit again? She'd written that piece months ago, but Sam possessed a reporter's instinct of committing the tiniest bits of information to memory. She wondered if he was conspiring with that tease on the street.

"Sam, I'm too old for games." He could play caring papa

if he chose, but she demanded treatment as an adult. Besides, she enjoyed watching him squirm.

"It's not easy"—he ran his fingers through his hair—"and it's not my business."

"Go on."

"I knew about you and Chelsea. I think love is love no matter—" He stopped and looked at Helen.

Outside of her parents, Helen had never outed herself to anyone straight before now. There were times in the past when straight friends asked her if she was gay, and she always answered honestly. Some stayed, some dumped her, but she felt clear to her bones that Sam was a stayer. Still, there was a quickening to her pulse, and she took a deep breath.

"Let me make this easier for you. I need to do something for the gay community. Something for myself." Her face was hot, but she survived her admission.

"You're going public, aren't you?"

"In some way."

"Why? They could stonewall you. Gays still get bashed, and the last thing I'd ever want is for you to get hurt."

"I'm tired of living underground. It isn't fair or healthy for any of us."

"I can't imagine what it must be like. I agree with you, but are you ready to risk your career?"

"There are laws to protect me."

"Laws schmaws. If the old geezers on the board want you out—"

"I hope the paper has the integrity to place merit over sexuality."

"Don't count on that." He looked squarely into Helen's eyes. "But you can count on me to fight for you."

"Thanks."

He rubbed a hand over his face and looked at the column again. "It's good copy." He nodded. "You're on for Friday."

"Good. Are we finished?" Helen stood, anticipating his yes.

"Not just yet." He waved her down again. "Let me read something, and I quote: 'Message to green eyes. I will have lunch at the restaurant that bears the name of the column we discussed. I'd like to talk with you further. Friday, one p.m.'"

Sam cocked his head and raised only one eyebrow. Helen let out a slow breath. She'd rather work the mailroom than lose the message.

"Starting a private dating service?" The editor was back.

"Sam, leave it in. It's a one-time deal."

"Lucky for you I'm feeling generous."

❖

Helen met Tucson at Central Park South for lunch. The weather was tauntingly warm compared with earlier in the week.

"Two pretzels with mustard," Tucson said and paid the street vendor. He handed one to Helen. "I can't believe you've never had a pretzel with mustard. Are you really a native of this smoggy city, or are you feeding us a load of bull in your columns?"

"To be honest, I grew up in Brewster, but you'll never hear me admit it in public." She bit into her pretzel and added a muffled comment. "This tastes pretty good."

They ate and chatted casually, but Tucson finished his lunch quickly.

"Now tell me, word wizard, what's with the column on closeted gays?" He dropped his napkin into the trash.

"Have you taken it upon your shoulders to help create a more accepting society for us?"

"I'm a realist. I'll never fully see that in my lifetime. I'm just tired of the oppression and I want to say something. My readers can interpret me however they choose, and they will."

"Well, oppression will always exist. We live with it and try not to carry a chip."

Helen stopped and grabbed his arm, not believing what she'd just heard. "How can you be so insensitive? It's attitudes like yours that give our society the notion that some are better than others. I've conformed long enough."

"You're turning into a martyr," he said, unruffled by her demeanor. "Talk is cheap. Coming out would serve a better purpose, but I don't see you jeopardizing your career."

Helen laughed to herself. The friend conspiring with the editor conspiring with the tease on the street. When they approached a vacant horse-drawn carriage, Tucson handed a wad of bills to a coachman and helped Helen up and onto the seat.

"What's going on that you hired a coach to smooth it over with me?" Helen asked as the carriage lurched forward.

"I'm leaving New York."

"Why?"

"For a job offer that I'd be insane to refuse."

"Just like that? New York's been your home for—"

"—thirteen years. I'm in a rut and it's time to move forward." He took hold of her hand. "I wish you'd do the same."

"Don't start with me. I have a terrific career and a roof over my head. Life is good."

"And memories. Don't forget memories."

The clop-clop of horse's hooves resounded like a finely

crafted timepiece. Helen listened while time surged ahead, while family, lovers, and friends took leave. The clock ticked and she sat comfortable on the second hand. Around and around and around, but she never moved a centimeter.

Suddenly, the horse reared, spooked by a careless jogger. The coachman regained control and the mare settled.

"Sorry," the driver said over his shoulder and continued his course.

Helen brushed bits of salt from her lap. "Don't tell me how to live my life."

"I'm not. I love you and I worry about you. That's all I'm saying."

Helen's eyes welled tears. "Will you please hold me?"

"Sure." Tucson pulled her close.

"I love you, too. I'll miss you. Will you spend time with me before you go?"

"You know I will. You're my best girl."

Helen laughed and wiped her tears with her napkin. "I'm your only girl. Will Pete go with you?"

Their ride reached the end and they exited the carriage. "Yeah. We've decided that happily ever after would do us good."

"Good. It's nice to have someone to grow old with."

Tucson slipped his arm around Helen's waist and they crossed Fifty-Ninth Street. "Yes, it is, and I want you to remember that."

When they approached the entrance to the newspaper building, a jarring jolt slammed Helen into a three sixty spin. Oomph! The thud of bodies and entanglement of limbs dumped a mound of mustard onto her scarf. Helen snapped when she recovered from the unexpected whirlwind.

"Damn it. Why don't you people watch where the hell you're going?" When she looked up, she caught her breath.

Once more, that woman stared back and Helen was lost in the loveliness of her eyes.

"Lady, jog in the park or something. Are you all right, Helen?" Tucson tried to wipe mustard from the scarf.

"I'm awfully sorry," Green Eyes said. "I hope you're all right, and I'll see that you receive a new scarf. Silk, I assume." She reached up and touched the damaged item. "Yes, of course." Her eyes shone happily when she looked into Helen's. Her cheeks were bright red. "We must stop meeting like this, Helen." The woman turned and continued her pace.

Helen was angry. A million and a half people in Manhattan and that same woman knocks her socks off a second time? She didn't buy it. She could sniff out a setup if it was buried fifty feet beneath concrete.

Helen shouted down the sidewalk. "On a first-name basis now? At least one of us is." But the woman was too far out of range to hear her.

"You know her?" he asked.

"Not really." She continued to look, hopefully to catch another glimpse of the black sweat suit and the tied-back hair that bounced across the woman's back.

"Helen, you're blushing."

"I'm pissed off," she shot back.

He laughed loudly. "No, honey, you're flustered. That woman does something to you. Admit it."

"Yes, she does. She annoys the hell out of me, as you can see by my scarf."

"Call it what you will, but I want to hear more about that chick before I leave." Tucson kissed her cheek. "I'll be in touch."

Numbed from the encounter, Helen entered the office building. She made a mental note to have Sam pull the message from the Friday edition. She had to maintain control.

Helen thought of herself more as an artist than as a writer. Anyone could write; few, though, could create effectively. Without creative control, she could become an assembly-line writer, grinding out books one month after a major story broke nationally. Helen would not accept a link to that category. She took pride in her investigations, her arousal of public interest, and made darned sure she could back up every word. No, Helen was not one to take assignments of the month, and Ms. Green Eyes seemed quick to become one of those assignments. Helen refused to oblige.

Her private life was safe now, powered by the past. Those she loved most dearly lay buried, deep in her heart. She loved her parents and Chelsea. Loved them totally; loved them hard. Now they were gone. There was no more love to go around.

With her scarf crumpled tightly in her hand, Helen approached the elevator. The woman's rosy cheeks and shortness of breath made their way into her mind again and stirred adrenaline.

The ring of the elevator bell sounded louder than usual. Bright aluminum doors opened wide. Several passengers hurried inside and brushed arms with those who exited. Helen hesitated, preferring to ride alone, but she gripped the scarf and stepped forward, into the mix.

Control was failing.

CHAPTER THREE

On Friday afternoon, inside the Black Sheep Restaurant, Helen swirled the ice of her White Russian with a stirrer. Ice chimed and clanged against the glass. She'd forgotten to have Sam kill the invitation, but no mystery woman had shown and the time was well past one thirty.

She looked away from the patrons. "If I'd wanted to humiliate myself, I could have disrobed in the display windows at Saks. That would be less embarrassing than publicly begging for a date," she said to the salt and pepper.

All of those people sitting around the restaurant knew she was stood up. Yeah, they knew. They glanced at her column on page four of their newspapers and then back at her. Some whispered and some smiled. Some she knew, and most of them gave her the "you poor dear" look.

Could she be any more brainless? If she never saw the woman again, that would be fine with her. But what if she did? How mortified would she be when the woman burst into laughter for not choosing to meet Helen? Maybe enough to reduce her to tears? Never. Maybe enough for Helen to fire back and grab those ample breasts that pounded into her each time they met. Would serve them both right.

Again, she looked down at the condiments. "I don't believe I did this." She'd let a little girl crush, the result of an overzealous imagination, run wild. "Crush? Grow up, Helen. I don't even want this sidestep from reality."

She paid the check and left.

❖

"Where to?" the cabby asked and looked into his mirror. "Hey. Aren't you the lady that wrote the column on queers? I think they should be lined up and shot."

Helen stared into the mirror. "What if you went home tonight and your daughter said, 'Hey, Pop, I'm a lesbian?' Would you shoulder the rifle, or would you prefer if someone else took a shot at her?"

"My daughter ain't no queer," he said.

"Don't be so sure."

"Don't be callin' everybody a queer."

"Just be quiet. I didn't ask for your opinion."

"I didn't ask for yours, lady."

"You damn well did if you read my column." After his attitude, she estimated hundreds of brutal calls and messages when she reached her office. "Look, buddy. I won't argue with someone whose grandest decision is whether to make a left or right turn."

"You got a smart mouth."

"Lately it's been rather dumb."

The cabby laughed and shrugged. "You ain't tellin' me nothin' I don't know. Now where to?"

"West Fifty-Seventh."

"What number?"

"Just go."

❖

After crossing the Avenue of the Americas, she had a short walk to her office. On a downbeat day, a casual stroll gave her a needed sense of relaxation before the onslaught of callers would damn her to hell, again.

An attack, indeed, but not of callers. Helen was shocked to witness a group of demonstrators, police officers, and television crews that had swarmed the entrance to the newspaper. Picket signs held messages from opposing groups. She presumed they were right wing Republicans whose slogans read: NO RIGHTS WHEN GAY'S NOT RIGHT and TEACH OUR CHILDREN FAMILY VALUES. Other posters, however, read: HELEN'S CLOUT CAN HELP US OUT and ABORT HOMOPHOBIA.

"No, it's not the opinion of the paper. Helen chooses her own columns," Sam told a reporter who shoved a microphone toward him. "But we'll defend the right of freedom of the press."

She hadn't anticipated a demonstration of public opinion. Phone calls from pinpricked patrons were easier to deal with. With reporters and cameras, there would be pressure to come out, and she didn't want to become a sideshow for the eleven o'clock news. At least not this way. She'd do that under her own terms. When she turned to walk away, members of the media snagged her, and she found herself no longer hidden from hungry and anxious ears.

"Helen!" reporter Jan Roland from NBC called out. She headed toward her, camera operator in tow. Helen watched Sam dash past them to be with her. Police held back the forty or so chanting protesters. ABC and CBS fell in with the NBC crew.

Sam took hold of her arm. "Are you okay to face the cameras?"

No, she wasn't okay. She'd rather turn around and make a mad dash for the Queensboro Bridge and then pick up a nine iron at the golf center in Flushing Meadows. It didn't matter that she didn't golf.

"I'll handle them."

Roland shoved a microphone near Helen. "You've stirred up the proverbial hornets' nest with your column," she announced to Helen and the camera. "Some of these individuals seem to think—"

"Tell her, Helen." A man waved a rainbow sign. "Come on. Tell her we're here, we're queer, and so are some of you." The chanting spread throughout the gay activists.

So cliché. Helen's eyes narrowed and she clenched her teeth. That type of finger pointing she loathed. She thought it obscene to incriminate others and, if forced, she would neither admit nor deny anything.

"My column supports the rights of a particular subculture of our society. I could have chosen any subculture."

"Baa, baa, black sheep. Have you any wool?" a woman and her female companion yelled.

Roland stepped closer with the microphone and Helen stepped back. "What do you expect to accomplish with your column?"

"Nothing. Unless our society is quick to emancipate their minds, nothing will change much. We're probably the only living organism that doesn't tolerate same-sex affection. And why is that? Is it because we have a brain with the ability to think and discern? No. Monkeys have those abilities." She looked directly into Roland's eyes. Helen had once dated the still-closeted reporter. "I suspect rats do, too." When Roland lowered her microphone and took a step backward, Helen pushed her way through the herd of protesters and cameras.

"Show's over," Sam said and guided her through the boisterous crowd.

❖

Alone, Helen stood at her office window and looked to the sidewalk below. The crowd had dispersed and she sighed wearily. She'd had the opportunity to speak out and it would be over. She'd be out of the closet and literally into the street. Bang. Boom.

To the pedestrians below she muttered, "Repetition. It's all you want. Why won't you allow us our choices? What scares you?" She looked at her reflection in the window. "What scares me?"

Freedom. Her right to choose. She knew, no matter how much she wanted freedom, she feared coming out alone. Helen had to organize her thoughts and plan, get them into action, and claim a fuller identity.

While New York's sky turned gunmetal blue, white headlights and red taillights clamored for position below. The time was past six and it had been one hell of a day. She ignored any messages that might be on her phone, preferring to deal with them on Monday. Her day was quiet now, and nothing remained to distract her. Sam dropped by and placed a box onto her desk.

"Reception sent this up. It's too light for a bomb. Good night, Helen." He turned to leave. "Good job today."

"Thanks."

Helen stared at the box. She'd often received tokens from readers and that one came as no surprise. Some people still appreciated her column. She picked up the gift and noticed the elegant wrapping. A shake presented a muffled sound. Curious. Suddenly, she remembered—mustard and silk. Her flesh tingled.

Alone with a cardboard container, which in no way, shape, or form possessed the ability to converse, Helen was speechless. She placed the package back on her desk and tried to justify not opening it. She knew the content, from whom it came, and that it was simply a replacement for damages occurred during an innocent, or not so innocent, jog. A scarf, but a scarf sent by a tantalizing woman she knew only as "yes."

Her fingers shook while she untied the delicate lavender ribbon.

"How appropriate."

Next was the creamy white paper.

"Virginal."

And finally, the box.

"Pandora's box." She took a breath. "Relax. It's a scarf. Just remove the cover…that's it…and now peel back the tissue. Very good, Helen."

And there it was: A scarf, red and silky. A promise kept. No ghosts flew out, no bugs jumped on her, no diseases wreaked havoc. Now pick it up.

She shook her head. "No, and I don't believe I'm having a conversation with myself."

Helen finally pulled herself together and picked up the soft and cool-to-her-touch garment. When she noticed another wrapped item, she tore through the tissue and her entire muscular system collapsed. Another scarf, as bright as emeralds. Beneath the layers of fabric, at the bottom of the box, lay even greater hope: a note. A name. Helen picked up the parchment envelope, removed the fold of paper, and read aloud. "My apologies for the accident and I do hope the scarves will make up for any problem I have caused. Of course silk. Could I have imagined anything less? Have a lovely weekend. C.C."

Frustrated, Helen picked up the green cloth and felt its gentleness. She touched it to her cheek and, once more, captured the delicate aroma of lily of the valley. She deeply inhaled a memory.

"C.C. That tells me a hell of a lot." She looked back at the note. "I can eliminate Carol Channing, Claudette Colbert, and Charlie Chaplin. C.C. Cynthia. Carol. Christine. I like Christine."

Once more irritated with the woman's elusiveness, and with her own obsessive curiosity, Helen shoved the scarves into the box, grabbed her belongings, and whisked herself out the office door.

CHAPTER FOUR

On Saturday morning, Helen snuggled deep into her down pillow and pulled the blankets to her neck. She stared at the old *Time* magazine cover she'd framed and hung near her dresser. The periodical date was October 14, 1991, and bore the headline "Jodie Foster. A Director Is Born."

On that cover, Foster personified sophistication. Amid a darkened background, a movie projector shone over her left shoulder, and her intense eyes studied the unseen screen in front of her.

"Not bad," she said and allowed herself the indulgence of imagining awakening to such a woman.

She studied the photograph longer. Finely carved facial features, sharp angles of cheek and jaw, all added depth to Jodie's eyes. Stacey had pointed out the small crease at the tip of the Foster nose. Stacey!

Helen tore her thoughts away from the image on the wall. Stacey. Last night. A dream. She thought harder. The club. Stacey had handed her a green drink. M something. A martini? A Manhattan? No.

All dreams had meaning. Helen threw back the blankets and grabbed the phone from her nightstand. She poked in Stacey's number.

"What?" Stacey growled.

"Good morning."

"Blondie?"

"I need to see you." Helen sprang from her bed and headed toward the bathroom.

Stacey groaned. "I just got in three hours ago."

"You can sleep later," Helen said and turned on the shower. "I'll be there at eleven." She adjusted the water temperature.

"Use your key," she grumbled.

❖

Stacey's apartment was located in what had once been a garment manufacturing building. The building now held private residences. She'd gutted the loft and turned it into an exotic showroom of thick carpets, mounds of prime-color pillows, foliage to make a botanist weak at the knees, and bright Warhol silk screens that lined the walls: Judy, Marilyn, Ingrid, Chanel No. 5, and more, but no Campbell's soup cans.

Helen closed the front door and headed for the kitchen. She brewed fresh coffee and, while Mr. Coffee completed his task, hand-squeezed eight oranges before she'd extracted enough juice and pulp for a decent serving. She wouldn't attempt that again for love, money, or even a Pulitzer Prize.

She'd purchased a yellow rose from a sidewalk vendor and placed the flower on the tray with her peace offering. At the bedroom door, she first peeked in to be sure Stacey was alone.

"Hey, you." No response. She entered the room and set the tray on a nearby chair and then sat on the edge of the bed. Stacey still gripped the phone and Helen returned it to its base. "Hey," she repeated and ran her fingers in quick patterns through Stacey's short, ash-blond hair. Stacey grunted.

"Why am I awake?" She rolled onto her back.

Helen pulled up the sheet to cover Stacey's breasts. "Because I need to talk to you."

"This is a nightmare." She pushed herself up and through sleepy, bloodshot eyes, focused on Helen. She managed a smile. "Blondie."

"I've missed you." Helen wrapped her arms around Stacey and squeezed.

"You just wanted to see me naked." She returned the hug.

"I've seen you naked. I wasn't impressed."

"No? Why not?"

"You have teeny tiny boobs."

Stacey let the cover fall away from her chest. She looked down at her breasts and pushed at the side of one. "Almost a C cup. They're good boobs."

"Teeny tiny. At least for my liking." Helen gave Stacey a quick kiss on her lips.

"Nice mouth. I can't think of a better way to wake up."

"You have no imagination."

"That's why you write and I run a bar." Stacey fell backward, onto the mattress. "Go away now."

"Get up, you bum."

Trying her best to rouse Stacey, Helen bounced and shook the bed, but hadn't expected to find herself suddenly flipped onto her back with Stacey straddling her and pinning her hands behind her head.

"I like this advantage." Stacey beamed as she looked down at Helen.

"You're the one without clothes. I could have my way with you."

"Take me. Break me. Make me a woman." She released Helen's hands and rolled to her back. "Please?"

"You know, you really are a pig sometimes." Helen slapped Stacey on the hip, but fully expected a comment of that nature from her. "It isn't any wonder you don't have a real relationship."

"I have lovers."

"But you never love." Helen stood and straightened her clothing.

"Look who's talking. You've been romancing Chelsea forever." She took quick steps to the dresser, grabbed a T-shirt, and put it on.

"That's different."

Stacey wagged a finger in front of Helen. "No no no no no. In our separate ways, we've locked our hearts." She spied the fresh orange juice and drank it quickly. "Thanks." She picked up the mug of coffee and Helen followed her out to a Plexiglas balcony. "So, Blondie, what's going on? We caught you on the eleven o'clock news last night. You looked pissed and petrified." She propped her feet on the railing and placed shades over her eyes. "And how about that Roland? You should have lip-locked her right there. She'd have passed out in an instant."

"Jan was never a good kisser, anyway. I felt like a damn hypocrite. Stace, I want to come out and I can't do it alone. You can help."

"How?"

Stacey's establishment, Xanadu, was located on the Upper East Side of Manhattan and was a popular hangout for the gay and lesbian elite.

"With all of those gay celebrities you rub elbows with at your bar. Think of how much weight it would carry if they could be persuaded to come out as a group."

"Are you serious? I know! I'll hold a debutante ball for all lesbians. You'll be the next"—she stressed the next word lasciviously—"*coming* attractions."

Helen shook her head but giggled the tiniest bit. "Do you ever stop?" In spite of herself, she loved Stacey and she'd have her no other way.

"Never. Cheap swine, I am. Always the animal." Always the colorfully correct dyke, she smiled proudly and adjusted her lavender sunglasses.

"In a sense, that's exactly what I want, but why limit it to women?" She raised an eyebrow.

Stacey looked over the top of her eyewear at Helen. "Oh. You're serious. Okay. I'm listening."

"If they would combine their talents and present a knockout show for one night only, where each would state their sexual preference, we could come out as a group. I would be their MC, of course. Simple."

Stacey abruptly pulled off her shades and stared at Helen. "You need a sedative. They'll laugh you out of the room."

"You aren't laughing."

"Your idea is preposterous, but it is something the community desperately needs," she said and put her sunglasses back on. "A star-studded event might help dispel some of the misconceptions of our community."

"Exactly. How many gay celebrities do you know?"

"Close? Fifteen maybe." Stacey rubbed her chin. "Some have big balls and might jump at a joint effort."

Helen's enthusiasm heightened. "Great. Can we use your club to get a group together for an initial discussion?"

"No. We'll reel them in here. They'll be more comfortable and there won't be any outside ears. When do you want me to herd them for a get-together?"

"The beginning of the new year."

"That's about twelve weeks away. Plenty of time to plan." She drank some of the now-cold coffee and grinned at Helen.

Lots of teeth and a mischievous smile. "I read your note to Green Eyes. Any response?"

Helen had become so caught up in their conversation that she'd forgotten that part of her life. Or maybe the woman wasn't even a part, only an irritation.

"She didn't show and I'm embarrassed. I sounded so desperate." Helen shrugged. "It doesn't really matter."

"You sell yourself short." Stacey opened a window panel and leaned on the railing. She looked to the street below. "Maybe she was out of town or didn't read your column."

Helen didn't comment. "I had a dream about you last night."

Stacey perked up. "Did you finally sleep with me?"

"Yes," she played back. "On top of both towers of the World Trade Center."

Stacey looked south, but the landmark structures were masked by lesser, but closer buildings. "Hmm. A little windy, but your choice could be interesting."

"My dream was you handed me a green drink and told me it was what I needed."

"Something with Midori, maybe," Stacey said, nodding. "Something right out of Oz." She turned to Helen. "That might match those elusive eyes. I'll be right back." After several minutes, she returned and handed her a color photograph. "Here's your drink. Take it slowly. No, in your case, you might want to chug that baby."

Helen reached for the photograph and her mouth dropped open. There was the jogger and Stacey cheek-to-cheek, grinning like drunken sailors at the camera. Before she spoke, she gazed long at her would-be assassin. Was that the woman who would reduce her to a puddle of pleasure? The one who would tear down thick and tall defenses?

"You know her?" Helen leaned forward on her chair and

stared at the photo. "You knew who I was talking about and kept your mouth shut? Jesus, Stacey."

"After hearing your description of her, I figured she was the one. You know I don't play matchmaker, but I'll stray from my policy a bit." She returned to her seat. "I don't want you to mourn the dead forever. Her name is Cory Chamberlain and she flew to Boston early yesterday. Otherwise, my bet is she would have met you at the restaurant."

"Cory Chamberlain," Helen said, and liked how the name felt when spoken. "What can you tell me about her?"

Stacey propped her feet up again. "Just about everything, but I won't say another word. That's for you to find out."

"Just answer one question: Do you have her phone number?"

Stacey breathed a heavy sigh, hoisted herself from the chair, walked back inside, and returned with the Manhattan directory. She dropped it not so casually onto the table. Helen jumped from the thud.

"Yes, and you do, too."

Helen considered the dense volume of pages in front of her. She refrained from touching it, as she had done with the box, but she knew that it held something that grabbed her attention and that was her fear of it. She estimated the weight of the book, and tried to guess on what page she would locate Cory's name. What page? Which seven numbers would bring Helen closer to giving life to the elusive "yes?" Reluctantly, she touched the cover but didn't browse the register.

"Still with me, Blondie?"

Helen looked away from the book. "Do you think I'm silly?"

"No. Things happen. Emotions stir and can fly into fitful directions. Sometimes that's good and sometimes it isn't. Cory's a damn fine-looking woman and she's obviously interested in you. She's charming, knows who she is, and she knows what she wants. You'll have to determine if the direction is good or bad."

"She sounds too good to be true. There has to be a catch."

"There could be. Somewhere down the line there are bugs in all of us."

Helen gave her a puzzled look. "And what are my bugs?"

"You've made mourning a profession and you annoy people in their sleep."

Helen put the corner of the photograph to her lips. "You've placed a shroud of mystery around her."

Stacey stretched and yawned loudly. "There's no mystery to Cory. Let's talk on Wednesday about your party. You'll have my undivided attention then."

"Do you think your friends might consider my idea, or are you patronizing me?"

She stood and pulled Helen up by her hands. Stacey hugged her tightly. "Don't even think about your party. Just go home and call that dame."

"Thanks. I'll think about it."

"No, Blondie, don't think. Just do it."

CHAPTER FIVE

Helen tried to convince herself that her anxiety was a girl thing, that time right before her period when she possessed enough energy to swim the Hudson and East rivers while towing a Circle Line Cruise ship. She ignored the fact that her hormones had ceased raging a week ago.

Surely a woman who maintained a teasing distance wasn't a cause for concern. It didn't matter that Helen thought "attractive" and "great breasts" each time they met. No, because Stacey's friend was toying with her. Dyke or not, that Chamberlain woman couldn't possibly be thinking the same things. Apart from all of the commotion, Helen wasn't on the market anyway.

To divert her restlessness, she frantically cleaned her apartment, labeled every neglected computer disk, alphabetically categorized her video collection, washed her hair, shaved her legs, and gave herself a complete manicure. With the final coat drying, the time was still only six o'clock.

"Now what? Clean the oven?" Not in this lifetime. "Paint the walls or shampoo the carpet?"

Perhaps she should burn her copy of Katherine Forrest's *An Emergence of Green*. That's what all that frantic cleaning was about, wasn't it? She wanted to forget that the color existed and forget that Cory Chamberlain was right there in the phone book. Right there. Stacey had sent her home with the photograph and she promptly shoved it into her own phone book. A face, a name, and now somewhere within those inches of paper was a phone number.

Helen sat restless in her chair and looked across the room to the Manhattan directory at the bottom of her telephone table. The intrusion seemed vulgar to her. Vulgar because it compelled her to snare the book, devour the number, and have it spit out again through her fingertips. Beep-beep-beep-beep-beep-beep-beep.

"Hello? Cory Chamberlain? It's Helen. Would you mind too terribly if I kissed your breasts for a wonderfully long time? Perhaps I could interest you in a playful romp through the sheets. What's that? Yes, I like that, too. Great. Meet me 'round the corner in half an hour."

Helen laughed at the absurdity of her imaginary conversation. She didn't chase women; she chased good columns and those wonderful Reubens from the New York Deli. Writing was safe; food was temporary. There was no loss, no death, nothing more serious to worry about than occasional retractions and lethal calories.

She fidgeted. She drummed her fingers on the fine oak grain of her Boston rocker; she tapped her foot to an unheard melody. She glared at the book and her blood tingled. The same tingle she had felt eons ago when she smoked cigarettes and knew when her nicotine level was dropping. It was as though her blood had turned into ants crawling through her, and it was then that Helen would know to light up. It was the only way to stop the jitters. She had to feed the addiction.

The voice inside her knew where to find the fuel. The voice that was Helen's, but it was deeper, insistent, and seductive.

Well?

Helen shook her head in annoyance. "Stay out of this."

She's a knockout, isn't she?

"What of it?"

She's been teasing you.

"Only once with the scarves."

She's teasing you.

Helen pursed her lips. "You sound like HAL from Kubrick's *Space Odyssey.*"

As HAL had control, I have control.

"And I don't?"

Remember the bath? That wasn't Chelsea.

"No. It wasn't." The swirl of her blood intensified. She closed her eyes and listened to her breaths. Slow. Deep. She remembered.

Lust happens.

She snapped open her eyes. "Not to me."

Liar. Pick up the book.

"No!"

You want her.

"I don't know her."

You want her. Feel the ants?

"Yes," she whispered.

Helen plopped herself onto the floor in front of the small table and yanked out the book. She took a quick glance at Cory's picture and set the photo next to her. She opened the pages directly at the C listings and scanned with her finger until she located three C. Chamberlains.

"You didn't make this easy, Stacey."

She dialed the first number.

"No Cory here," the first person said.

She dialed the second.

"You have reached the residence of Carl and Jessica Cham—"

She hung up and her blood pulsed quick time through her veins. Helen wrote down the third number, placed it into her pocket, and closed the book. The photo remained untouched.

"This is silly." She shoved the book under the bench and headed toward her bedroom. "I don't chase women."

She cleaned the bathroom next. What a wonderful idea. Such a great Saturday Helen had as Suzy Homemaker. There was nothing quite like cleaning the toilet with the vengeance of a jackhammer. Don't be alive. Be a martyr. Remember the Alamo. If we don't remember the past—

But she did remember, and she permitted it control. Would tears for the dead be her life forever? Surely there was more, and she pushed up from her knees. In the mirror was the Helen that had known more. Touching and laughter had once existed. Hugging. Making love. She missed sharing hot cocoa on snowy walks through Washington Square Park and the feeling that living was a good thing.

She looked to the wall on her right. If she'd had X-ray vision, she'd be staring at Cory's photograph. That woman. The body that slammed into her more than once. How fulfilling it felt having a woman—

"Damn it!" she shouted and slammed the can of Scrubbing Bubbles onto the back of the toilet. She thundered into her bedroom and grabbed the phone. "So I'm chasing a woman."

She pulled the paper from her pocket and punched in the digits. When she remembered Cory was in Boston, she relaxed. There would be no live voice contact and she could leave a message. She found control. In the middle of the second ring, their phones connected.

"Hello."

Helen froze; a thud pounded in her chest. Damn it.

"Hello?"

Briefly, she moved the receiver to arm's length, took a

deep breath, and let it out. Slowly, she brought the phone back. "Cory Chamberlain, please," she managed to say.

"I'm Cory."

Here she is, Helen. The tease. Make it good.

She waited an eternity of five seconds. "You set me up!"

Okay, dummy. What the hell was that?

"Who is this?"

"Helen Townsend." She thought she could hear a smile form on the other end. "I'm sorry. My social graces take a hike when they encounter you." She heard a slight laugh.

"I believe that was a compliment. How are you, Helen?"

"A nervous wreck."

"Your honesty is intact," Cory said with quiet composure.

"Am I disturbing you?"

"Not at all. I'm thrilled that you called. I was just cleaning my aquarium."

Cleaning? They certainly had at least one thing in common. Helen listened so closely that she didn't realize it was her turn to mumble a syllable or two. The air was quiet until Cory broke their silence.

"Has grace taken a sabbatical again?"

Helen faltered and then answered. "Yes, and I feel foolish."

"Don't. It's a pleasure to hear your lovely voice."

Although it shouldn't have, with Cory's not so subtle ways and words, her flirtation surprised Helen. "You're very bold, Cory Chamberlain." She hesitated. "Are you bold enough to see me tonight?" There. You did it.

Cory's response came instantly. "Yes."

Helen felt in control again, and all that remained was to say when and where. "How about my place at eight?" she said with all the impudence she could gather. "My address is—"

"I know where you live," Cory said. "I talked to Stacey an hour ago. She said you might call."

"Well, then—" Caught off guard, Helen fumbled for words. "Uh, yeah, bring popcorn." She hung up the phone without saying good-bye. "Bring popcorn? Oh my God."

CHAPTER SIX

The time was five minutes to eight when Helen finished applying her mascara. With what felt like nothing but five thumbs on each hand, she smudged her way through two tissues and several profane words before she claimed victory over the brush.

"Done."

She approached a floor-length mirror. To keep the evening simple, she chose tan slacks and a deep brown, oversized sweater. Comfort would help her through the evening but when she looked into the mirror, she was horrified.

"Damn it. I look like a root beer Popsicle." The doorbell rang and she threw her hands up in resignation. "Why would I think any of this would be simple?" She pulled on one shoe and immediately tore it off. "So I'll be a comfortable Popsicle."

At the front door, Helen watched through the peephole. One by one, a slow striptease, Cory pulled at her fingertips and removed the first glove.

"Look at you," Helen whispered.

Now was her deciding moment, but which decision would hold more regret? If she didn't open the door, she could remain safe in her sparkling apartment and work-oriented life. That would serve Cory right, more than Helen, but sending her home would even the score, in Helen's mind. Or she could open the door, which provided no more promise than a solitary bath. Promises. She wasn't looking for them, but a growing part of her yearned to meet the future and what it could present.

Just as Cory rang the bell again, Helen stepped back from the door. She looked at the lock and placed her hand on the doorknob. She grasped the deadbolt latch and waited. Before her inner voice kicked her in the pants again, Helen turned the lock and quickly opened the door. There they stood with nothing but a simple threshold between them.

Cory raised her head and reached down to the bag beside her. She raised it to shoulder height.

"Popcorn delivery," she said with a wide, half-moon grin.

Helen smiled and a new feeling overcame her anxiety. The feeling was bliss. "I never turn down popcorn. Please come in." She reached for the bag and closed the door behind them.

"Hello, Helen." Cory removed the other glove and extended her hand. Gently, their fingers grasped. "I'm Cory Chamberlain."

With Cory's tender squeeze, she became real for Helen. No bodies collided, and no one ran in the opposite direction.

❖

Helen sat comfortably on the sofa. She peeked into the bag and giggled like a ten-year-old when Orville Redenbacher smiled up at her.

"What is all of this?"

"You said to bring popcorn and I wasn't sure what kind you liked." Cory reached into the bag and introduced the items one by one. "We have Jiffy Pop, microwave with or without butter, and this bag has different-colored kernels." Helen laughed at the assortment that Cory piled onto her lap. "This one gets popped on the cob and here's one popcorn ball. I don't care for them." She seemed pleased at Helen's amusement. "Pick your poison."

"You're too much."

Cory leaned back onto the sofa and crossed her legs. She looked elegant in her black pleated slacks and white crepe blouse. A delicate gold necklace hung gracefully at her throat. There was a small charm that Helen couldn't identify from her distance, and Cory's rich brown hair hung loosely over her shoulders. A wisp of bangs fell over her forehead. Helen noticed a slight overbite that shaped Cory's mouth to tantalizing, kissable perfection.

Feeling awkward with their first real meeting, Helen opened with small talk.

"Your name is interesting. Is it short for Corrine?" She pulled her legs under her, in keeping with her comfort theme.

Cory shook her head. "I was named after a county in Texas."

"Really?"

"It's true. My parents lived in Coryell County. A small town called Copperas Cove."

"Coryell. I like it. It flows nicely. Mine is forceful. It's too harsh."

Helen couldn't believe the verbiage that her brain voluntarily blew through her mouth. Certainly, somewhere along her life, she had learned to structure a meaningful sentence of more than three words.

"Helen's a lovely name." Cory smiled. "Tell me about yesterday's column and the black sheep one. You sound like a woman with a plan."

Right to the point, just when she thought Cory might become a bit more veiled with more than a few seconds in Helen's presence.

"Well." Helen fidgeted with the ear of popcorn. "I hear over and over that much of the entertainment world wouldn't exist if it weren't for the talents of the gay population."

Cory nodded. "I believe it's true."

"I'd like gay Hollywood, any gay celebrities, to get their act together, so to speak."

"Come out together, you mean?"

"Yes."

"A group thing is unprecedented," Cory said. "We need more names out there."

"Could you come out in such a way?"

Cory thought for a moment. "I could, providing I had a lover."

"Why would that matter?"

"It would be important for me to say 'Look, world, I'm in love with this fabulous woman.' I'd want to show all that she means to me, to everyone around me."

Helen sat in silence and studied Cory's eyes. Looking for evidence of color-enhanced contacts was closer to the truth, but she found her eyes to be quite real, as real as her words. Cory charmed her, and her intuition said that Cory Chamberlain was no phony. She stared long and hard.

"Hey, you," Cory said with an air of seduction. "Vacationing again?" She reached for Helen's hand and slipped her fingers beneath it. Helen smiled but pulled away, not wanting the ants to awaken. Cory withdrew her hand, reached into the pocket of her slacks, and took out a plain elastic band. She pulled her hair together and secured it behind her. Helen saw she missed some strands. With quiet restraint, she didn't reach over to tuck them behind Cory's ear.

"I've been wanting to meet you," Cory said, pushing back the loose strands of her hair, "but I wasn't sure how to go about it." She looked to Helen for a reaction.

"So you ambushed me." She kept a serious face, all the while wishing she hadn't let go of Cory's hand. "You could have called my office."

"Yes, but what do you say to someone who doesn't know you?"

Helen nodded. "I'd say 'hello' and introduce myself, but your ambush worked. There was an immediate intensity to your way. You left me with that huge question of 'is she gay?' After that you just annoyed me."

Cory laughed. "I'll tell you honestly that I planned our first encounter, but running into you while I jogged was an accident. I felt badly about your scarf."

"You've made good on the scarf. More than once, if I remember correctly." She looked over at the piano and hoped Cory wouldn't see how the box of scarves sat there and remained untouched from the day she received them.

"And have you found the answer to your question?"

"Yes, I have," Helen said.

"Good, and I didn't assume incorrectly about you?"

"You did not," Helen said. She smiled at their stuffy speech.

"Even better, so I'll just throw this out there for you. You're wonderfully attractive."

Helen hadn't heard words like those in years. They landed on her ear with a sweet ring, but they also stirred memories of Chelsea. The words made her sad and her feelings must have shown on her face.

"Did I overstep a boundary?" Cory asked.

"No. You reminded me of something. It's been...I don't know." Helen shrugged. "It's been a while since I've taken interest in someone, so I get weird around you."

Cory shifted her position. "Then let's forget that part," she said, "and just be people." She looked around and spied the old, well-kept upright piano that was tucked into the corner of the room. "That's quite an antique. Do you play?"

Oh, damn. Cory couldn't help but see the haphazardly thrown box. She'd think Helen was unappreciative.

"No, I inherited it from my grandmother. I can read music, but my left hand has a mind of its own. My only keyboard action is on my PC. Fortunately, the keys are closer together." She suddenly remembered her manners and a smooth diversion might work for the neglected gift. "Would you like a drink or something?"

"Tea would be nice."

Helen stood. "We'll make some of this popcorn buffet you've brought."

Cory rose from the sofa and stood face-to-face with her. The ants started marching again, up Helen's legs and right into her scalp. Fast, itchy little suckers that sent a shiver through her. That had to stop. Helen let go quickly of Cory's hand.

"Would you feel better if I leave?" Cory asked. "We can get together another time."

Helen's eyes widened. No, she'd feel worse. "It's not you," Helen said. "It's me." She cringed internally. She was an award-winning writer and those were the best words she could call up? Helen thought. *It is you, damn it. Your beautiful eyes, your lovely mouth. Just let me have a tiny taste of your lips.* She leaned closer to Cory.

"Relax. Music soothes the soul. Would you like me to play for you?" Cory asked, walking toward the piano.

There was no mistaking the presence of the haphazardly tossed box of scarves, when she looked back at Helen and smiled.

"I'm sorry. They're lovely, really. I just haven't put them away."

"It's okay." Cory pulled out the piano bench and sat.

"You play?" Helen found herself beside Cory again.

Cory nodded with a gleam in her eyes. "I've been known to dabble. Have any favorites?" Helen sat next to the piano, facing the bench. She watched while Cory played three scales. "The tuning isn't too bad. I have a flexible repertoire. What pleases you?"

Cory pleased her. Just sitting there, with her hands sliding across the keys, that pleased Helen. "Play something you like," she said.

"I'm a lover of romance," Cory said and began to play.

Romantic it was. Almost any song Helen had ever loved flowed from Cory's fingertips: "Lara's Theme," "The Shadow of Your Smile," "Fly Me to the Moon," and others. A medley of Arlen, Berlin, and that oh-so-romantic Cole Porter. "I've Got You Under My Skin." Ants, maybe? There was no mistaking that she wooed and flirted with her songs.

Cory closed the cover when she finished. "Feeling better?"

Helen nodded. "You're good. Come on." She stood and led Cory into the kitchen. "You've earned that tea."

At Cory's suggestion, they used the fireplace for making their popcorn. She put on the teapot while Helen rummaged through the cabinet for cooking oil. Together they cleaned the popcorn basket and prepared the fireplace for initiation.

"Why have you never used this fireplace? They're great for cold New York nights." Cory pushed up her sleeves and then wadded paper that she tucked beneath the logs.

"Like tonight?" Helen opened a tall tin of matches, removed one, and struck it on the slate. She held the small flame to the papers until they caught fire. "I don't do much entertaining," she said and threw the match onto the logs. She looked back to Cory. "I associate fireplaces with romance. Not much of that flying around these days, either." She placed the roasting basket on the hooks.

Cory sipped her tea. "Will you tell me what happened?"

"I was with my last lover for three years and then she died from cancer. Everything happened quickly. She never had a chance and I never prepared for the worst. I became a workaholic and an emotional invalid." Helen stretched onto her side and studied Cory. "Chelsea's death crippled me. That's why I react so oddly to you. Everything inside is shifting gears."

"We share somewhat common ground." Cory placed her cup on the saucer beside her. "Women have used me for my talent." She positioned herself to face Helen and Helen propped herself up on one elbow. "Do you mind if I sit closer?"

"It's okay. Tell me what you do." Helen chipped at the clear nail polish on her thumb.

"I'm a musician," Cory said. "I'm hoping to connect with a group in Boston." She touched Helen's hair, and her fingers grazed Helen's neck. "And I'd like to connect with you."

Helen's internal voice, the one that damned the negative and grabbed the obvious good with gusto, kicked in.

She's at it again. How can you resist her tender touch? Come on, where's that hopeless romantic? Listen to me: Go for the necklace.

Cory turned slightly and the firelight bounced from the gold charm at her throat. It beckoned Helen to move closer. She pushed herself up on one hand and reached for the charm. Cory bent forward to meet her hand.

"This is lovely. Very delicate. It's a musical note." Helen was delighted with it. "You take your music seriously." She felt the silken flesh of Cory's throat, warm against her fingers.

"A sixteenth note, to be exact, and yes, I take my music very seriously." Cory cocked her head to one side and studied Helen's face, inches from her own.

"And your women?" Helen looked into Cory's eyes.

"You make it sound as though they're lined up outside my door." Cory looked at Helen's mouth. "I'm selective."

"And have you selected me?" The question was gutsy. It sat on the edge of vanity, but was brave nonetheless.

"Yes." She touched Helen's cheek.

"Why?"

Cory placed her hand on top of Helen's. "I admire the way you talk to the city. When we came face-to-face, you took my breath away."

Whether "took my breath away" was merely a line or the truth, Helen was—she stroked the golden note—charmed.

"And now?" She let go of the necklace and placed her hand on Cory's shoulder. She watched her lips.

"Your lips are so close to mine," Cory said.

The reality of their nearness shocked Helen and she backed off. "I'm sorry," she said, flustered. Then, having noticed that Cory hadn't moved away, Helen sat upright, moved closer, and slid one hand behind Cory's neck. The tease would pay for the ambush. "No, I'm not sorry." She stroked, and her fingers absorbed Cory's heat. Cory closed her eyes. Helen spoke softly. "I haven't kissed a woman in three years."

Cory opened her eyes. "That's a difficult statement for me to live up to, but I'll try." She cupped both hands gently around Helen's face and pulled her close to her mouth. Their eyes held and Helen felt Cory's warm breath on her lips. "You needn't wait a moment longer."

Helen drew a nervous breath at the first touch of her lips. Their softness infinite, Helen pressed harder, taking Cory's lip between hers. As she gently kneaded the warm, precious flesh, Helen felt Cory's tongue slip softly across her lower lip.

A log crackled, crumbled, and settled, supported by stronger logs below. A burst of heat flowed through Helen.

She opened her lips and was overjoyed when the sweet fullness of Cory's tongue glided past with slow, deliberate strokes. Helen could taste lemon and honey from Cory's tea.

Is this so difficult, Helen? Feel the energy. It swirls around you. She feeds you, this woman who is so alive in your arms. Let go, Helen.

Helen coiled her arms slowly around Cory. She pulled her closer and not close enough. Cory stroked Helen's back, her sides, the back of her neck. She pressed against Helen. Breasts to breasts, Helen thought she would stop breathing. In a panic, she pushed away. A wet smacking sounded between them and Cory's eyes fluttered open.

"I'm sorry," Helen said. Her body trembled. Before Cory could respond, with what Helen hoped would be a word or two of reassurance, the moment was shattered.

Pop! Pop pop! Pop! A kernel hit Cory in the face, another whizzed between them, and then a sudden barrage of the tiny treats hurled themselves toward them. Helen laughed when one stuck to Cory's lips.

"The cover!" Cory shrieked, pointing to the basket cover propped against the hearth. "Quickly!"

In a fit of laughter, Helen lunged for the top, only to drop it into the fire when she tried placing it over the pan of projectiles. "Damn it. Now what?"

"Duck." Cory laughed and eagerly placed some popped morsels into her mouth.

Helen scooped a handful from the carpet and threw it at

Cory. "You're a lot of help." The barrage continued until she placed the screen in front of the wholegrain attack. "Oh God." She waved her hand, trying to rid her space of the stench of burning popcorn. "That's the worst smell ever."

Glancing at the avalanche that surrounded them, Cory continued to eat happily. She pointed to Helen's sleeve. The loose fibers of her sweater had created a Velcro effect and Helen's left side was nearly covered with popcorn. Cory reached over and plucked a few of those pieces off. She ate those, too.

"You look lovely in white," Cory said. "You'll make a stunning bride."

Helen sat back, shook her head, and sighed. "Ten thousand unemployed comedians and I get you." She scooped another handful of the popcorn and tossed it at Cory.

Cory's kiss blasted her into a physically unstable realm. The kiss had been of nuclear proportions, with no time given to question its authority. Fission had neared fusion, and surely she'd have become liquid if the kiss had continued.

"Do you want to talk about it?" Cory asked, a grin still on her face.

"About what? Popcorn or my rampant hormones?" She pulled the popcorn from her sweater and Cory assisted.

"I don't regret kissing you." She popped a few pieces of the corn into Helen's accepting mouth. "Let's consider it a prelude." She brushed the final pieces away from the sweater.

Some prelude. Would her finale be as strong? Would her hands execute the silvery notes of romance and cause Helen's body to scream the passion of a ballad? Maybe her lovemaking would be endless?

There it is. There's the romantic side of you.

Helen blushed. "I just need to slow down."

"Understandable." Cory playfully flicked a piece of

popcorn from the floor and toward her. "Why don't we clean up this mess?"

❖

Cory waited by the opened window when Helen returned from putting away the vacuum.

"Come here," she said over her shoulder. "I want to show you something. Turn out the light."

Helen turned off the light and joined her. "I'm game." She leaned on the windowsill.

Cory pointed into the night sky. "Between the roof across the street and that big star, can you see the tiny constellation? It's like a little kite."

Helen blocked the city light with her hand. "Yes, barely. I can see seven stars."

"It's called Delphinus. It's simple to our eyes, but if you look at the same constellation with a small telescope, you can see hundreds of stars within. They're actually beyond it. It's breathtaking if you don't expect it."

"But when you look again it loses luster." Helen sounded disappointed.

"But you have choices," Cory said. "Don't look at it ever again and remember its effect, or always look at it as though it were the first time."

"Or get a stronger telescope and look deeper," Helen said.

"Very good." She nudged her. "You're an explorer."

"More like a nosy journalist." Helen gave her a quizzical look. "Is there a moral to your story?"

"There are surprises in life and what we do with their effect is entirely up to us." Cory looked at her watch. "It's getting late."

Her response sounded cryptic, but Helen was about to make a choice without giving it or the stars a second thought. She pressed a kiss to Cory's shoulder and then looked into her eyes. "I want to see you again."

"Is tomorrow too soon? Come for brunch."

❖

Cory jotted her address on a piece of paper and Helen slipped it into her wallet. At the door, she faltered. How do you say good night when you've just met, yet shared a kiss with enough passion to erupt popcorn? Or so it seemed.

"Good night," Helen said as she hugged Cory.

"See you tomorrow."

CHAPTER SEVEN

Tucson called the following morning. Helen pushed her morning coffee away and leaned back into her chair. She couldn't believe what she'd just heard.

"What do you mean you're on your way to Seattle?"

"We decided to sublet the apartment. We've packed a few essentials and we'll get what we need when we find a place to live."

"Can you stop here first? I want to see you and Pete."

"No, honey, we're already in Pittsburgh."

"Damn it. You said we'd get together."

"I know. I'm sorry, Helen."

Their abrupt departure disturbed her, but she couldn't stop them from leaving. At least they weren't dying and would be a phone call away. Without asking, she knew he'd be back in town for an occasional function. If they were happy, she was happy, too.

"I'll miss you, Tucson. Call me, okay?"

"You know I will."

"Oh, wait. Do you remember the woman that slammed into me and ruined my scarf?"

"Yes."

"We had a date last night, and I'll see her this afternoon."

Telling him felt right and she felt good saying the words. She had taken a new beginning.

"That's wonderful news. We're about to enter the tunnels, so I have to go. We love—" Their connection was cut off.

Helen washed her breakfast mug and dressed for her second get-together with Cory.

❖

"That's the Dakota." The cabby handed the paper back to Helen and then pulled into traffic. "Have you there in no time."

Helen looked back to the handwriting. "The Dakota," she said quietly.

The residence wasn't merely another apartment building in just another neighborhood. For Helen, mention of the Dakota conjured up flashes of Central Park West, John and Yoko, Lillian Gish, and Rudolf Nureyev, to name a few. A gnat's eyelash away, in the San Remo, lived Mia Farrow, but gone were the days of Woody Allen. Money and fame had resided on Central Park West, along with history and headlines.

❖

Cory greeted her at the door and whisked her into the kitchen. Helen looked around the large room. An ensemble of copper-clad pots and pans hung from the ceiling, crowning a butcher block and sink. Each cabinet door was clear glass and every item was orderly. And tile! White tile from floor to ceiling gave the room a sterile feel.

"I apologize for being abrupt. I have to get this off the heat." Cory scurried to the stove, lifted a kettle, and poured its creamy white, rich soup into a serving dish. She covered it and turned to Helen. She let out a quick breath. "I'm glad you're here. Hungry?"

The tang of sour cream hit her nostrils and Helen nodded quickly. "Yes. You cook? That's something I have no talent for."

Cory's sweat suit lent sensuousness to her swagger as she walked toward Helen. She laced their fingers together. "Where does your talent lay, Ms. Townsend?" Cory teased and kissed her cheek.

"All dormant," she said and matched the kiss.

On cue, her hyperactive mind kicked in and discharged a volley of electrical impulses through her brain.

What's dormant? The kiss? The bath? Remember the bath, Helen? Those eyes that penetrated your thoughts and hurled you into the most exquisite—?

Enough. The room suddenly became too warm for Helen. She cleared her throat with that same pathetic sound she'd made during the ambush. She backed away.

It was then that she noticed an alcove and dining table. That niche wasn't as medicinal, with its walls stripped of tile. Instead, small pears and peaches were clustered on wallpaper with a golden-yellow background. The space felt cozy, and Helen envisioned a comfortable breakfast there.

The small table was perfectly set with crystal and silver. In the center, a small assortment of fresh fall mums burst with colors of red, orange, and yellow, their colors embellished by streaming sunlight.

"Is all of this for me?" she asked.

"All for you." Cory looked toward the table and back at Helen. Her bangs had loosened and she looked adorably impish. "Pretty, isn't it?"

"Beautiful."

Over soup and salad, they discussed Helen's research on

the Third Reich and her interest in German-occupied Poland. Her intention was to write a book on the ghettos of Warsaw and Lodz and the death camps, primarily Auschwitz, Dachau, and Buchenwald.

"I had planned to travel to Auschwitz with my father, for hands-on research, but then I shelved the book."

Cory munched her salad. "Was that when Chelsea died?"

"No, years before her death. Solidarity and Lech Walesa were coming into power and the entire Eastern Bloc was experiencing dramatic change. Travel there wasn't exactly safe."

"I've been to Poland," Cory said as easily as another person would say they'd been to Philly. "It's a remarkable country with a fantastic history. They have quite a love for their country. After the war, the old city of Warsaw was rebuilt through photographs and works of art." Cory rattled on. "The Black Madonna…"

Her remark surprised Helen. Nobody "goes" to Poland, and nobody says it's a remarkable country with a fantastic history. Forever, Poland has taken the brunt of ethnic jokes.

Helen wiped her mouth with the napkin and then placed it neatly on the table. Remembering the vastness of Cory's residence and the fact that she'd seen no piano while she shuffled through, she felt uneasy. Who was this Chamberlain woman? She eyeballed her with suspicion.

"Were you visiting the country?"

"I traveled there for business first and then pleasure." Cory stood and began clearing the table.

Used by women. Secretive. She's a spy. For us? For the KGB? She's a Commie. A pinko. A sympathizer. Who else would infiltrate Poland on business and then pleasure? Sure, overthrow a country today, feast on its bounty tomorrow. The nerve. But where did the piano come in?

"Wait," Helen said. "There's something I don't understand. What exactly *is* it that you do?"

"I travel," she said. "A lot."

"So will you answer my question?"

"Yes." She sat quietly for a moment, almost as though she weighed her answer. "Come with me." She took Helen by the hand. "I haven't been totally up front with you, but it comes from my insecurities." Cory led her into the living room and stopped in front of large oak double doors. "This is where I leave my vanity."

She opened the doors and Helen stepped inside. Cory stayed at the threshold, leaning against the door, her arms crossed. Helen slowly walked around the room.

Framed posters occupied most of the white wall space. She read them aloud: "Chamberlain Plays Chopin. Two nights only." It was from a recent Carnegie Hall date. Then, "Cory Pops With Boston," a Boston Pops guest appearance. One poster displayed a photograph showing only Cory's eyes, with the remaining features in shadow. Helen wanted to touch the poster but didn't. She continued to read the placards that sent her around the world: London, Paris, Berlin, Rome, Warsaw.

Cory rustled at the doorway and Helen continued her survey. Finally, she walked to a grand piano that faced a wall whose windows held no drapes. Cotton clouds and blue sky reflected clearly from the top of the ebony instrument. She touched the polished finish and noticed, in another corner, a life-size porcelain statue.

"Apollo. The god of music," she said.

She attempted an abrupt about-face, but still another item on the wall stopped her. There, in a black frame, stood Cory and her delicious half-moon grin, shaking hands with Queen Elizabeth. Beside the photograph hung a framed program. Helen read the entire page. "By Royal command, in recognition of her outstanding contribution to the arts, Coryell Chamberlain performs Brahms and Borodin, in the presence of Queen Elizabeth II, at The Royal Albert Hall, eight p.m. on August twenty-first, nineteen ninety-four."

Helen completed her about-face and glared at Cory. "You were commanded by the Queen? Well, isn't that special?" Helen scoffed. "Doesn't that make you a knight or something?" She stepped up to Cory. "Are you trying to make a fool of me?"

Cory stood erect, surprised by Helen's anger. "No. Helen, I—"

"When did you plan to tell me? You said you're a musician and I'm thinking, okay, a local with talent, but this—" She glanced around the room, shook her head, and pounded out, through the double doors. Cory followed.

"You don't understand. Let me explain."

"Do you know how foolish I feel? You're an international celebrity and I didn't recognize you. Obviously, I've had my head up my ass for three years, but you didn't have to keep this from me." Helen found the kitchen and grabbed her jacket. She turned to Cory. "I prefer honesty to half-truths."

"Helen, performing for the Queen was a great gig. It doesn't mean—"

"Last night I marveled at how real you were." She looked into the eyes that began to pull her under again. Along with her anger, she felt arousal, which left her with two options: either get the hell out of the building or begin to remove those sweats that looked adorable on Cory. Helen hoisted her pocketbook over her shoulder. "I'll find my way out, thank you."

Pushing past Cory, she wouldn't look at her. Embarrassed, she wanted first to run hard and then deal with the anger.

"Wait," Cory said as Helen blindly made her way toward the entrance. "Let me explain."

"You have nothing I want to hear." She closed the door

firmly behind her, loud enough that it echoed in the hallway. "'A musician,'" she said sarcastically and entered the elevator. "'Known to dabble,'" she mocked. "All of a sudden I have fucking nobility on my hands." She pounded her hand against the back wall of the elevator. "Damn it. I never say that word."

The Carnegie Hall poster, those green eyes. Helen thought she'd probably passed the music hall a dozen times while those eyes watched. She remembered the poster now, the way Cory seemed to beckon her. She'd never given those eyes a second thought. That would have been a slap in the face to her devotion to Chelsea.

Helen hurriedly walked the distance to Lincoln Center. She sat at the edge of the fountain and pigeons gathered around her. They cooed and seduced her for a possible meal.

"Don't tell me," she said to the feathered creatures. "You're really doves incognito." She reached toward a bird that had ambled close to her feet. "Don't be afraid," she said, and the bird took flight. Helen leaned her elbows on her knees. She buried her face in her hands and tried to justify how she felt.

What are you afraid of?

"She lied to me."

She didn't. She is a musician.

"She held back. I don't like her ways."

You like pain?

Helen looked at the granite walkway beneath her feet. "I'm fine."

You're a spider web. The dead cling to you.

She looked at the steps across from her. "How can I trust her?"

She meant no harm. She's been used.

"I won't be her savior."

You could be her lover.

Helen bit her lip. "There's plenty of women for her to lure into her life."

Don't be afraid.

"Of what?"

To admit how lonely you really are.

Helen wanted to cry. Not for half-truths but for the three years she'd lost. Dead time. Safe time. Now this woman had barged in and slammed her life into a tailspin. She spiraled downward, faster and faster. She closed her eyes. Tears spilled from them.

"I am lonely." She wiped the tears with her palm and breathed a sigh of relief.

Intimacy was a ghost for her. Sex had become four minutes of self-gratification on the nights when she had felt emotionally close to Chelsea. And now, this woman, this Cory Chamberlain, had her feeling that another human's touch had no equal.

No equal. She wondered about Cory's breasts. She could feel their smooth curves warm her cheeks and palms, could feel them pressed against her own breasts. She laughed at the irony, remembering her inability to structure a proper sentence in Cory's presence and realizing that now she wanted nothing less than to feel all of Cory against all of herself.

"Okay, Townsend, settle yourself." She took a deep breath and looked around the outside of the performing arts center. "Now what do I do? Go home and clean something? Oh, I'm getting awfully good at that. The whole place looks like the Ajax white knight moved in."

Helen cringed and groaned. "Damn it. Knighthood is reserved for Englishmen. I know that. I don't even know if the Queen still does it. Of course she does. Maggie Smith, Anthony Hopkins, Paul McCartney." All wore the modern title of Dame or Sir. "Cory must think I'm an idiot." Helen pushed herself up from the fountain. "Well, little birdies, I've my intelligence to prove."

She made a single phone call before leaving. "Hi, it's Helen Townsend. Can you have the *Princess* ready in a few hours?" She looked at her watch. "Four sounds perfect."

❖

The return walk to the Dakota afforded her time to pull her emotions together. By the time she reached Cory's door, she felt more comfort with the direction she was about to take. She knocked softly on the apartment door.

"It's open."

Helen opened the door. "You don't say that in New York and survive," she said in warning, and closed the door behind her.

Crouched in front of the aquarium, Cory swung around, lost her balance, and fell to her knees. She blushed, then smiled bashfully. "I've misplaced my social graces as well. I had a feeling it was you."

"Proper position for a knight to greet her lady." She dropped her pocketbook and jacket to the floor. She approached slowly and knelt in front of Cory. Her eyes never strayed from Helen.

"It was a Royal Command Performance." She took Helen's hand, brushed her lips across the fingers, kissed the tip of her thumb. "Knighthood is reserved..." Her voice mingled with the soft sounds of a bubbling aquarium.

"I know," Helen said. "I came back to...to tell you..." She moved forward and nuzzled Cory's ear. "You're a tease." She bit into Cory's neck. "An attractive, soft, warm, and wonderful tease." She licked the abused flesh.

"No." As Cory pulled Helen's mouth close to her own, her eyes searched Helen's. "This is real."

Their mouths came together. Cory's tongue slid deeply into her and Helen hungrily captured each stroke. Her hands swiftly traveled over Helen's breasts, down her sides, and beneath her sweater. Her fingertips painted lightly over Helen's belly while warm lips rained kisses onto Helen's face.

"Come to my bed," Cory said.

"No." Helen released Cory's hair from the elastic and gathered it into her hands. She nuzzled the cool thickness, breathed the lilies. "I want you here. Right here in front of the fish, but not now. Not yet." She moved away and took a deep breath. "We're going for a ride."

CHAPTER EIGHT

W here are we heading?" Cory asked while they sped along I-684.

"Westchester County Airport."

"Oh. Is someone waiting for you? If I'd known you had other plans, I would have invited you for another day."

"No other plans," Helen said. "There's something I want to share with you."

"Okay." Cory turned in her seat to face Helen.

"How was your trip to Boston?"

"Perfect. The Pops pianist had taken ill and they called me to cover for him. I always have fun with that group. I was also asked to conduct two pieces." She held her arms in the air and motioned a down beat. "There's nothing like conducting a group of talented musicians."

"Multitalented, huh? I have to admit that I don't own any of your recordings." She pulled into the airport. She hadn't been there in months and it was time to spread her wings. "Follow me," she said when they left the car.

A short walk later, an airport official met Helen on the tarmac.

"It's good to see you again, Helen. The wind is a little tricky today, but I don't think it's anything you can't handle." He took the pre-written flight plan that she handed him and tucked it into his jacket.

She grabbed Cory's hand. There was a hesitation to Cory's step as they followed him to a white Piper Tomahawk. On the side of the fuselage was the word *Princess* painted in pink. "She looks great, Bill."

"The mechanics checked everything and I took her on a trial run. She's purring like a kitten."

Helen ran her hand along the propeller of the single engine plane. "Thanks," she said and turned to Cory. "Ready to go for a ride?"

"You're a pilot?" she asked.

"Taught to fly by my father and I was licensed at eighteen. Come on. Let's have some fun."

Bill assisted Cory onto the wing and buckled her into the copilot seat. Helen visually inspected the outside of the plane. After determining that all was safe, she hoisted herself onto the opposite wing and climbed inside the cockpit. She was proud to share this time with Cory, and it felt like a playful "look what I can do" after seeing Cory's music room. Not that she needed to get even, she only wanted to feel special, something more than a writer for a newspaper.

Helen turned the key, and the single engine coughed and the propeller finally spun on the nose of the plane. She adjusted her headset. Each gauge showed the proper reading and the gas tank registered full. She checked the position of the flaps.

"Good afternoon, control tower. This is KNP twenty-three ninety. Do I have a clear runway?"

"KNP twenty-three ninety, this is Westchester tower. You're clear for runway two. Repeat. You're clear for two."

"Thanks, Westchester," she said and maneuvered the plane into position. Cory watched every move she made. "Why so quiet?"

"I didn't know if I should speak."

Helen laughed. "It's okay. It's not like we're heading into

the night for a secret bombing mission. Let's get into the air. We'll talk there." She adjusted her mic again. "Tower, this is KNP twenty-three ninety and we're ready for takeoff."

"KNP twenty-three ninety, this is Westchester. You have a nice tailwind for takeoff. The sky is yours. Have a great flight, Ms. Townsend."

She powered the throttle and the Tomahawk roared as it picked up speed down the runway. Around 800 feet, she pulled back on the control and the *Princess* climbed into a cloudless blue sky. After she arced the wings toward Connecticut, Helen leveled off at 8,000 feet and set a cruising speed of 100 knots.

"It's a beautiful day," she said and removed her microphone.

Cory glanced around the panel of switches and lights. "Don't you have to set vectors or something? Coordinates? How do you know where to go?"

"We'll just cruise the Berkshire Mountains. They're kind of like up the block. They're familiar." The plane was jostled by light turbulence and Cory gripped her seat. "It's a little windy." A stronger bounce rocked them and Cory turned ashen. "It's okay," she reassured her. "I'll take us up a little. The air might be smoother." She reached for the controls but Cory stopped her.

"No. Not higher." She grabbed Helen's hand. "I have a fear of flying. I do it a lot, but I usually take a sedative first." Frightened eyes stared into Helen's.

"Oh my God. Why didn't you tell me? I'd have never made you go through this." She took hold of the controls just as the plane hit an air pocket. The drop lifted Helen against her belt and the plane plummeted several feet. When Bill mentioned the wind, she wished she'd cancelled the flight, but pride had stopped her.

"Oh, Jesus. Helen!"

"We'll be okay. We're going back." Strong wind pounded the aircraft and Helen looked over at Cory. "There's a bag to your right, if you need it." The plane dropped again and Cory grabbed the bag. Helen put on her headset. "Westchester tower, this is KNP twenty-three ninety. The wind is kicking us around and we're returning for landing."

The plane continued with fitful rocks and dips during their flight. Once more, the Princess dropped and Helen cursed the turbulence. She hated wind when flying and understood the horrors it could present. She was once a passenger with her father when they were snatched from the sky and forced to make an emergency landing in a rocky field. She tasted the terror of grazing a grove of trees and not knowing if the landing gear was intact. Her father had handled the plane through to an abrupt stop, but the force had broken Helen's leg and her father's wrist. It could have been much worse.

On her approach to Westchester, the wings tipped left and then right, but she brought the plane in like the professional she was. When the landing gear hit the runway, she sighed with relief.

"We're down," she said and made the short taxi back to the tarmac.

"I'm sorry I spoiled your day," Cory said before they exited the plane.

"You spoiled nothing, but you should have told me of your fear and I shouldn't have assumed you wouldn't mind flying." She nodded toward the bag. "Still empty, huh?"

"Fortunately." She unbuckled her seat belt. "Can we leave now?"

"Yeah."

❖

Cory's color came back and she was calm in the car. Helen nearly laughed when she remembered how quickly she'd snatched the barf bag from the door. At the same time, she was thankful she didn't have to break out the cleaning products.

"I guess we threw each other a curve today," Cory said. "It's beyond terrific that you're a licensed pilot, but I don't know if I'd ever be able to share it with you."

"Ah, that's okay. I can't play a piano very well. That kind of evens us." She took hold of Cory's hand and rested both on the gear shifter. "Look, don't hold back on me in the future. I can't read your mind."

"I know." She turned to Helen. "Will you come home with me?"

"Yes, but I insist on cleaning our brunch mess while you play something classical for me on your piano." She turned off the parkway and onto Seventy-Ninth Street.

CHAPTER NINE

Cory had just completed a short classical piece when Helen placed the final dishes into the dishwasher and wiped the counter. She grabbed a chrysanthemum from the vase and joined Cory at the piano. She placed the flower atop the instrument. Cory smiled up at her and continued playing.

"Do you like this?" she asked Helen.

"Yes. It's romantic."

"I wrote this when I was in the seventh grade. My music teacher loathed it."

"He or she had no taste, then. Have you composed more?"

"No." She finished the song in the upper register. Sounds that mimicked wind chimes surrounded Helen. "Composition is too difficult for me. I'd rather play or conduct." She walked to Helen's chair and sat on the chair arm. "My next solo appearance is tomorrow, in Buffalo, and then I'll do a two-night show with the Lansing Symphony Orchestra on Tuesday and Wednesday." She twisted Helen's hair with her fingers.

Her touch was sensuous, something more than "Hello, it's nice that you're visiting with me." Helen's flesh warmed too quickly to her liking. She stopped Cory's hand, but another part of her wanted her to continue. That simple touch awakened more of her than their kiss had done.

"If you're trying to seduce me, it won't work," Helen said.

Cory only smiled her beguiling smile and said nothing more. She stood up, pulled Helen to her feet, and walked out of the room alone.

Helen stood staring at the large doorway. Was she supposed to go with her? She certainly didn't want to look like a needy puppy that followed her mistress everywhere. She waited and took a closer look at each poster and then the picture of the Queen, before Cory called to her.

"Helen?"

With her answer now clear, Helen returned to the living room. Cory sat on the floor, watching the aquarium fish. She turned to Helen and extended her hand. "Come here."

"Are we about to perform some type of spiritual relaxation thing by watching the mollies?" She sat on the floor beside her.

"Spiritual? I hope so," she said and ran her hand along the back of Helen's neck. "I'd prefer if no fish were involved."

When Cory's hand drifted to the center of Helen's back, she closed her eyes and thought of nothing more. The touch was dreamlike and one she didn't want to awaken from.

"We don't know each other," she said but made no attempt to end Cory's freshness. Soft fingers now stroked gently at her cheek.

"And this is me, being honest. I want you. Right here in front of the fish, just like you said."

"I suppose I'm another girl in another city for you." Helen opened her eyes and Cory leaned closer. Her lips tickled at Helen's ear, and the reaction drifted to her breasts. She agonized between submission and slapping Cory. "You probably have a global harem. Your touch is tender. Do your other women tell you that?"

She laughed softly and moved her hand away. "There are no other women."

Helen looked down at the hand she wanted against her for a long time and then looked into Cory's eyes. "I want you, too. Right now. I don't care if we met five minutes ago."

Stretched among discarded clothing, Cory's soft curves tantalized Helen. "Your breasts"—she stroked their sides and lingered over dark nipples—"are unbelievable." She watched their fullness rise with each breath. Cory quivered when Helen took a nipple between her lips.

"Troy fell for the beauty of Helen," Cory said and gently rolled Helen onto her back.

Cory was fire against flesh. Fueled strokes of her tongue ignited Helen's wrists and palms, made their way behind her knees, and circled her ankles. Helen twisted and arched her seared body. Her throat crackled and strained for air that fed only the consuming blaze. Her breasts were a scorched sanctuary where Cory would retreat and recharge, only to repeat her sweet burn of loving.

With final tenderness there, Cory pulled her mouth from Helen's breast. She gathered Helen into her arms and kissed her powerfully. Helen strained against her, aching for that final touch. The touch Chelsea had never granted her.

Helen swallowed, caught her breath. Cory's eyes burned feverishly. A split second of doubt flashed through Helen's mind as an old memory returned to haunt her.

"Please, Chelsea," Helen pleaded.

Chelsea argued. "It isn't sanitary. I'm sorry, Helen, but I just can't do it."

"Then let me. I crave you, Chelsea."

"If you must, but don't kiss me afterward."

Helen's insistent mind snapped her back to reality.

Don't be afraid.

"Now?" Helen breathed hoarsely.

"Yes." Cory licked across Helen's mouth, kissed her way downward, across her breasts, her stomach. Helen felt the slightest tickle of Cory's lips against her hairline. "Now," Cory whispered.

Helen's eyes shot open, her lungs sucked a quick gulp of air. "Oh—Mmm," she cried when the silk of Cory's tongue glided gracefully through her. Helen felt fingers enter teasingly slow and wonderfully deep.

The intensity of Helen's orgasm flashed between thighs and brain. Sparks that flew from her depths turned into pounding strobes behind her eyes. Brilliant crystals burst into raging flames. Her body was steel and felt feathery light. Feathers and steel, crystal and flames, Helen finally shattered, fragmented from the explosion within.

Cory rested her head on Helen's thigh and caught her own breath. Helen watched her fingers sift through soft hair that, she was certain, must tickle her nose. When Cory's breaths came slower, Helen reached toward Cory's shoulders.

"Come up to me, baby," she whispered.

Cory leaned over, kissed the wet curls, and stole a final taste. Helen raised her hips—a kiss returned.

"Hi, baby," she said as Cory stretched on top. "Mmm," she murmured, pulling Cory's mouth to hers. A loving kiss. "Your mouth smells like almonds."

Cory looked down at her. "You taste like almonds. You taste wonderful."

Helen licked slowly around Cory's mouth. "Lightly salted," she added. She was then quiet. Instead of words, she wanted to please, and tease, and make love to this splendid naked woman in her arms.

From the top of Cory's head to the soles of her feet,

Helen turned dry into wet, all the while turning wet its wettest. She kissed Cory's eyes, her throat, and found a wonderfully sensitive area behind her left knee; the place where she would return to hear the soft groan that escaped Cory. Helen feasted on large breasts and generously bathed her face with them. She bit into soft arms, sleek calves, and tender thighs that lured her to their center.

Three and a half years since she had last made love, five years since she had last tasted a woman. Helen closed her eyes and gripped Cory's hips.

Is this what it takes, Chelsea? Do I let go by having something we couldn't have?

Helen opened her eyes to be sure the woman she held wasn't Chelsea. Beyond the sloping stomach and rounded breasts, Helen saw Cory watching her, waiting, welcoming her. Cory reached to Helen's temples and pulled her closer.

"Please," Cory whispered.

Helen breathed the rich, flowing scent of her. Cory's ready lips glistened. Helen grazed them with her mouth and Cory twitched, moaned her pleasure, raised herself in search of Helen's mouth.

Helen pressed into the wetness and could taste her, a flavor for which she had never before found a definition. She tasted again. Rhine wine and champagne burst in Helen's mouth, zipped through her bloodstream, and jolted her brain.

With her tongue wide against the wetness, she traveled the length of Cory. She explored, selfishly savored every warm drop until satisfied. Only then did Helen move higher.

Cory was helpless to resist the quick sensations. Helen pulled Cory's clitoris gently with her lips. She tormented the muscle with long strokes and then swift flicks that made Cory's hips jerk with each tap. Helen felt shock waves ripple through

Cory's legs and out through her toes; up her torso, out from her fingertips, and into Helen's cheeks. As quickly as Cory sounded them, her impassioned cries slipped into soft sobs.

"It's okay, baby." Helen soothed and kissed as she cradled the trembling Cory. "It's okay."

"I couldn't control it." Cory took a deep breath. "So quick."

"So good."

Helen stroked the length of Cory's hair. Cool tears kissed Helen's shoulder. She ran her hand over the smooth curve of Cory's side. Down over her hip, around to her back. She listened to gentle breaths of her new lover drifting into sleep.

"You purr like a kitten, safe in my arms. I could fall asleep to your gentle lullaby."

She pushed Cory's tangled hair away from her cheek and whispered, "Do you know what you've done?" She brushed her lips against Cory's eyebrow. "You've shown me how to feel again." Helen moved her finger lightly down Cory's nose. It twitched. Helen smiled. "You'll pay for this, my sweet sleeper."

For three years, Helen had made no attempt to pull herself out of her emotional nosedive. Finally, and without further hesitation, she let go of Chelsea. She kissed Cory's lips and savored her smooth form against herself.

There would be no crash and burn. Filled with life, but just a little bit sleepy, she closed her eyes and drew Cory closer.

Helen embraced joy.

❖

From the gentle bubbling of the fish tank, coupled with the feeling that she was the prime target of intense eyes watching her, she awakened. Cory leaned on one elbow and draped a leg over Helen. Her free hand rested near Helen's neck.

"I feel wonderful," Helen said, revitalized from a deep sleep. "Was I out long?"

"Forever," she said and kissed the tip of Helen's nose. "A few minutes. You're a fine lover."

"I lost my breath once or twice, too." Helen shivered, looked around. The kitchen door was to her left and the hallway to her right. She then looked back to Cory. "I think we're naked in the middle of your living room." She turned her head to look above and behind her. The aquarium continued its uninterrupted bubbling, and the fish seemed attentive to their presence. She grinned. "They saw the whole thing. Look at them with their tiny lips making big and little ohs."

Cory laughed. "I was making them, too." She rounded her lips and worked them quicker than the swordtails.

Helen threw her arms around Cory and squeezed. "Mmm, yeah. I remember."

Cory's eyes continued to sparkle, but her expression became serious. "I want more than one night."

Helen reached beside her and grabbed the wrinkled sweatshirt. "You should have given thought to that before all of this."

Cory nuzzled between Helen's breasts. "Really, Helen. What do you want?"

She pulled Cory's hair away from her shoulders and ran her fingers over them. "A blanket, a hug, and time with you, baby."

Cory popped her head up. "Be right back," she said, and Helen watched her scamper down the hallway. Her size seven butt twitched this way and that. Cory was wiry, full of quick and precise movements that measured well against the precision she must display as an accomplished pianist. And accomplished she certainly was. But despite the posters from all around the world that hung in Cory's music room, she'd made mention of a group she was looking to connect with in Boston. What more could she want?

Dragging three comforters and with two oversized pillows jammed beneath her arm, Cory reappeared. Two of the comforters became their first bed together. Under the third, they snuggled.

"What is it you want to do in Boston?" Helen asked after a long kiss from Cory.

"Conduct the Boston Light Orchestra," Cory said proudly.

"Really? I thought you were a solo act. World-class. Why would you want to give that up?"

"I want stability. I want to grow old with someone. I've experienced too many coattail relationships. Some women would have dumped me in a minute if I had a finger amputated."

"Not all, I'm sure."

Cory became quiet. Helen saw a distant look that seemed like a love from long ago. She allowed her the time to reflect, and Cory soon shook off the thought.

"Who was that?" Helen asked.

"Sorry."

"It's okay. Tell me about her."

"Elinor was my first lover. I was twenty-one and she was thirty-two."

"A cradle robber. What happened?"

"My music got in the way. I was never there and our breakup was ugly. She got physical and I walked out."

"She hit you?"

"She threw my piano bench at me. I was amazed she could

fling it so quickly and so far." Cory laughed, but the hurt was obvious.

"And that was that?"

"For a while. After some time, I called her. We yelled a lot and she asked me to come home."

"Did you?"

"No. I couldn't give up the music."

"A career move," Helen said, trying to soften Cory's action.

"At her expense."

"What about your expense?"

"It's made for a lonely life."

"Have you and Elinor made amends?"

"We're long-distance friends. She lives happily in Baltimore. We connect every so often."

"And now you want to settle down?"

"I'm tired of dashing all over the globe. Kirk Janssen is leaving the Boston orchestra in April, and I've made it known that I want his position."

"Then you've had experience."

"Especially with Boston. Kirk likes my style, and the musicians and I click."

"I don't see how Boston can turn you down, then."

"Well, they can. I just have to wait."

It disturbed Helen that Cory's time would be so limited. Would theirs be a weekend relationship? The paper was in New York, the conductor's baton was in Boston. Helen dismissed the thought. Already she had them married, mowing the lawn, and squabbling over wallpaper.

Well, hell, she thought. This could be more than a wham, bam, roll in the hay. Give it time, Helen. Let love happen. Sometimes love prevails.

"You're a scary old broad, Martha," Helen said.

"And you're a thief. Dudley Moore. *Arthur.* Right?"

Helen stuck out her tongue and pulled the comforter to their necks. Cory leaned into her shoulder. Within a loving embrace, they were ready for sleep.

"To hell with the Queen's rules. You'll be my knight," she said just before she dozed off.

Cory looked up at her. "And you my lady."

Softly, they kissed. Soundly, Helen slept.

CHAPTER TEN

Although she hadn't the power to resist Cory's charm, Helen had the decency to wake up in her own bed on Monday morning. Thoughts of Cory, and not visions of Jodie Foster, encouraged a smile that hustled her happily into a new week. There was a column to write, a meeting with Stacey on Wednesday, and a Friday dinner and theater date with her very own concert pianist.

Dressed, ready to make her entrance into a new week, Helen looked at Chelsea's photo. A twinge of guilt tugged her heart, but tears no longer fell.

"I like Cory," she said to the photo. "I'll never forget you, but I want this change in my life." She removed the photo from the frame and placed it inside an old picture album. She dropped the frame into the garbage and headed out for the day.

❖

Her week at the office proved full speed ahead. On Wednesday, the hour neared five p.m., and she'd just completed the editing on her newest submission, when her private line rang.

"Hello," she said.

"Good morning, Ms. Townsend. I'm taking a survey on your activities from Sunday afternoon," Cory said, business-like. "If you choose to participate, the questions will take only a few minutes."

Helen laughed softly. "Okay, shoot."

"On a scale of one to five, with five as the best answer, how would you rate my ability not to grab the controls of the airplane and drop us out of the sky?"

"That's a seven, easily. You were the consummate overachiever."

"Question number two: If you hadn't made love with me, would you have the longing with you daily?"

In truth, she'd felt naughty when Cory outright said she wanted to sleep with her. Naughty in a nice way. Naughty in an I'm-so-glad-you-told-me-so-I-wouldn't-embarrass-myself-by-jumping-your-bones kind of way. Yes, she would have given plenty of thought to sleeping with her, but Cory didn't need to know that.

"I'd give that question a low four."

"Hmm. My plane paralysis gets a better rating, huh?"

"Courage is much more admirable than lust."

Cory exaggerated a sigh. "I think that places me somewhere between the Cowardly Lion and the Mayflower Madam."

"You could do worse. Are you in Lansing?"

"Just arrived at my hotel. There was a message waiting from Liz, my manager. I've been asked to guest conduct the Toronto Symphony on Thursday and Friday."

Helen frowned. "Oh. Toronto sounds like a nice addition to your Boston résumé." That response was more appropriate than "What about our date?" She was disappointed, but there was no reason to rush their relationship any more than they had.

"I'll be home Saturday afternoon. Can we plan something for that evening?"

"Sure. Give me a call." She looked at the clock on her computer. "I'm heading over to Stacey's for supper. Have fun tonight."

"Thanks. We'll talk soon."

Their conversation had ended and Helen looked forward to planning a party.

❖

Stacey stretched onto her sofa. "I can't guarantee a hundred people, but I know of a few who will come to your shindig." She bounced a Nerf ball from Warhol's silkscreen of Ingrid Bergman.

"It's a start," Helen said. "Maybe word of mouth will bring in a few more."

"I like the idea of a variety show, and there we have it. Party planned." Stacey sat up and threw the ball at Helen. "Now tell me about Cory." She wiggled her eyebrows.

"Uh, what about her?"

"You've had these cute little smiles pop up all during our conversation and I think Chamberlain is the cause of them."

Helen took a breath. She'd thought Stacey would have missed those moments when Cory snuck into her mind. Was it the moment when she remembered having her breasts massaged while Cory nuzzled between her legs? Or was it the time Cory's tongue moved slowly down Helen's back? Her hormones stirred at both thoughts; she smiled again and then looked at Stacey.

"We spent some time together this past weekend. We went flying."

"Uh-huh. Maybe you did, but I think you got laid, too."

She laughed and childishly stomped her feet on the floor when Helen didn't respond. "You did! Oh my God, this is wonderful. No more Chelsea."

Helen shook her head in disbelief of her actions, somewhat embarrassed. "I barely know her and I didn't try very hard to say no."

"It didn't kill you. You're consenting adults and sex is fun. Are you two an item?"

"I want to see more of her. We'd made plans for Friday, but already she's had to cancel. It makes me wonder if that's how our relationship would be."

"Maybe that's her bug. Her schedule is crazy, but if you can pin her down, I think you're in for a treat. She's always been among my favorite people, and no, I've never slept with her."

"That's good to know. All right, no more talk of her." She threw the ball back at Stacey. "We've agreed on food and alcohol, so keep me posted if your friends bail and I'll try to come up with another idea."

Stacey walked her to the door. "I love you, Blondie," she said. "I'm so glad you've shed your mourning clothes."

"Me, too. Both of those."

CHAPTER ELEVEN

Three weeks into December, and Stacey's words had rung true. Cory was rarely in New York, and Helen relied on mutual phone calls from there to as far away as Singapore. She received flowers two days a week, and once Cory had sent a signed compact disc of her music. "The beginning of your Chamberlain collection," her handwritten note had read, along with "I miss you."

Helen often stayed at the Dakota apartment, mostly for its proximity to the newspaper, and also to see if she might feel comfortable living there, had the topic ever come up. Cory had even opened a small room for Helen to have as a work area.

When Cory was home, Helen was happiest. The CD became obsolete when she sat and listened to Cory play. There was nothing sweeter than having a private pianist at her fingertips, sometimes literally.

"You have a floater," Helen called to her. She reached into the aquarium and scooped the red, scaly corpse into her hand. "I thought you bought time-released food blocks."

"I forgot to put one in the tank," Cory yelled from the bathroom. "If you would stay here when I'm gone, they'd have a better chance of survival."

"That's some mommy you have," Helen said and tapped

food into the tank. Three remaining fish ate heartily while she wrapped their dead brother with a tissue and joined Cory. "Here." She held out the small wet package.

"I don't want that." She pushed her hand away with her elbow and continued to floss her teeth. "Toss it in the disposal."

"You can't just grind him up. He's got family in there!"

"Then flush him."

Helen looked into the bowl of blue water and shrugged. "Bon voyage." She pressed the handle and dropped him into the swirling abyss. "I don't understand why you have the aquarium if—"

"It was a gift, and not one that I think about. Like someone dumping a puppy at your front door."

"I hope you'd feed a puppy."

"Of course I would, but I'd also find it another home."

"Then find a home for the aquarium."

"Do you want it?" Cory asked and Helen shook her head. "I thought not. Nobody wants the aquarium and it was, as I said, a gift. I shouldn't give it away."

Helen slapped Cory's backside. "Then get your act together and take care of them."

"I guess you have an act to put together, if those Hollywood heavyweights latch on to your show." Cory dropped the used floss into the trash and then swished a mint wash through her mouth.

"It'll be a challenge."

Cory spat out the wash and rinsed with water. She turned to Helen. "You have the drive. I imagine there is very little you can't do."

Helen smiled lovingly and wrapped her arms around Cory. "Do you feel better now that your teeth are clean?"

Cory grinned like a chimpanzee. "Much."

"I'm glad you're home." She gave her a playful bear hug.

"Me, too. Maybe someday you'll move in with me?"

"I don't know. I'm here when you are."

Cory checked the temperature of the Jacuzzi. "You're punishing me, aren't you?"

Helen began to strip and Cory assisted. "Why would I do that?"

"For my not being here." Cory turned on a CD player. Beethoven's "Moonlight Sonata" played softly.

"I didn't say that."

"You said 'I'm here when you are,' meaning I'm not here." Cory let her robe fall to the floor.

"I love your shoulders." Helen ran her hands across them. "They're perfectly straight."

"Unlike your answer," Cory grumbled.

"Well, you aren't here, baby, and I do spend time here, but I can be alone just as easily in my own apartment. Besides, I sometimes work in the room you opened for me. I'm just not responsible for the fish." Helen slipped into the bubbling tub.

"But it's not home to you?" Cory turned the lights low.

"No. Not without you. With you, maybe the Dakota will be home in the future. Not now."

Cory lit several candles, placed throughout the bathroom, and lowered herself into the Jacuzzi. Helen, her face damp from the misty water, wrapped her legs around Cory's waist. Vapor surrounded them and she splashed warm water over Cory's breasts and gazed at her shapely body that glimmered in the orange glow of candlelight. Raised and mingled from their flesh and bubbling water, curly wisps of steam became a dance of spirits.

Helen stretched her arms and steadied herself on the edge of the fiberglass tank. She relaxed her legs and released Cory.

Helen's body floated upward in offering. Cory ran her hands along Helen's exposed thighs, through thick curls, over the smooth belly, and grasped the swell of breasts.

Cory whispered, "You're beautiful." She pinched tightened nipples and Helen's body tensed with shock. Cory gazed into her eyes. "Tell me what you want." A bead of water ran down her cheek.

Helen released her grip on the tub. She lowered Cory onto the water's surface and supported her back. Cory's thick hair floated, a silky seaweed beneath her head. Helen took Cory's breast into her mouth, gently sucked, and then with more greed. She rocked Cory's body in rhythm. Water lapped steamy waves over Cory's flesh.

"That feels wonderful."

Helen pulled her mouth away and kissed her lips. "I went home the day we met"—she fiercely licked Cory's nipple—"a hot bath"—she waved the water over Cory—"filled me with desire for you." She looked deep into Cory's eyes. "I closed my eyes and saw you." She ran a hand over Cory's slick belly, and then pulled Cory's hand out of the water. She kissed each finger.

"I wanted you then," Cory said.

Helen placed Cory's hand on the swirl of hair. Cory pulled it away. Helen took her hand once more and held it there.

"What?"

"Shh." Helen's breaths shortened. "Feel what I felt." She massaged with Cory's hand. "Want me and have only yourself." Helen pressed the fingers into Cory's ache.

Cory whimpered. "I can't."

"You can, baby." Helen kissed her. "Just look at me. Watch my eyes." She began a slow circling with Cory's hand. Cory closed her eyes. Helen commanded her. "Look at me, baby." Cory's eyes opened halfway.

Helen watched driftwood take shape, molded from erotic waves. When Cory's hand found a rhythm all its own, Helen let go.

"Is this what you want?" Her hips joined the rhythm.

"Yes, baby." Helen watched, content in seeing Cory pleasure herself. "You're lovely. Feel how wonderful your body is to me." Her eyes returned to Cory's and she reached and pressed the hand harder. "Let me see you."

"Kiss me," Cory breathed.

Helen pushed her tongue deeply into Cory's mouth. Her own body now energized from the heated waters and sweet sounds that emanated from Cory. Helen released Cory's hand and moved hers lower. She pressed her thumb deeply into her.

"Oh," Cory gasped and trembled through her torment. "Harder, Helen." She quickened her private massage.

"Yes, baby." Helen's breathing stole Cory's rhythm. She pushed her thumb deeply, pulled slowly out, and then entered Cory again. Helen stayed to the depth of her, and rocked Cory against the hand.

Cory came with the power of thunder. Her vibrant body stiffened and released. Wisps of steam danced a ballet while crystalline music from Cory's throat echoed within the walls; powerful sounds that traveled the length of Helen's body like heated mercury and choked her with her own desire.

❖

Helen turned the bed lamp off and swung beneath the blankets. She could just make out Cory's moonlit features. She was the Carnegie poster come to life, but Helen couldn't see the color of her eyes. She pushed Cory's bangs away from her forehead.

"Tell me about your family." She moved onto one elbow and Cory rolled onto her back.

"Mom and Dad live in Dallas. They stayed in Texas after he retired from the service."

"How many years?"

"Thirty."

"What are they doing now?"

"Mom hangs with the girls and brags about her kids." They laughed. "Dad owns a small farm equipment repair business. I haven't seen them in a year. When I play Dallas we get together."

"And your brother lives in London?"

"He's a broker for the London Stock Exchange. He likes rain and stress."

"Any skeletons in the closet?"

"Just me, but we don't talk about it."

Helen nodded. "My mother knew, but I could never tell my father, and I was closer to him."

"He probably would have loved you all the same."

"I'll never know."

They listened to the quiet. Helen ran her fingers through Cory's hair. She treasured their quiet moments. There weren't enough of them.

Cory suddenly broke the silence. "Have you ever smelled the rich farm soil in Texas?"

Where did that come from? "I've never been, and I don't particularly care for the smell of dirt."

Cory pushed up on one hand. "This isn't just dirt. It's so rich and fertile it invades your senses. You know that land will produce. I could be a farmer."

Helen laughed. "You? Your job is to slay dragons for me and the Queen, note the order, please."

"I could change my profession."

"Change is good. It's a learning experience."

Cory smiled triumphantly. "I'm glad you agree. Now think about moving in with me."

"You little sneak!" Helen collapsed onto the bed.

Cory laughed. "You're so easy."

"As you are," Helen pointed out. "Like your episode in the Jacuzzi." She mocked Cory. "Oh! Mmm! Ah!"

"I faked it." She snuggled into Helen's arms and gave a soft sigh. "I've never done that on request," she said with an embarrassed laugh. "You have an interesting power over me."

"Not power. You trusted me and you were fantastic." Helen kissed her mouth. "Thank you."

As they nestled, Helen closed her eyes. She muttered, "A farmer. Right."

CHAPTER TWELVE

Many of Stacey's friends agreed to a private get-together. Helen was nervous about how they would receive her idea, but the good news was Cory was in town. If the night turned into a shamble, she'd be there to lick Helen's wounds.

"Your guests will arrive soon." Among mosaic mounds of living room pillows that surrounded her, Stacey raised her wineglass toward Helen. "I admire your courage, Blondie."

"Courage?" Helen sipped and leaned against the bar.

"Spunk. Guts. Balls." Stacey shrugged. "Whatever you call it, you have to convince the cream of the entertainment world to show their true colors. Not an easy task."

"That doesn't bother me." She waved her off and studied her drink. "Reporter and celebrities. That's a potentially volatile mixture." Helen laughed. "They'll probably take one look at me and head out the door." She motioned a U-turn with her hand.

"I doubt it, Blondie. Otherwise they wouldn't come." Stacey pushed herself to her feet and returned to the bar for refills. "They trust me. The only bitchy one will be Blair and, if I funnel her enough Scotch, she won't care if Rush Limbaugh's here." She handed Helen the full glass and made a toast. "Success."

Helen nearly choked on the wine when the doorbell rang. She checked the position of her belt and tried to smooth her skirt, but static wreaked havoc and the skirt became more like Saran Wrap. She struggled, powerless against the clinging mess.

"Quite a predicament you're into there. Wet towel, then a gin and tonic," the guest said and caught the cloth when Stacey flung it from behind the bar. "Let me help."

Helen's eyes caught the pitch-black hair of the newly crowned Queen of Broadway, Marty Jamison. Helen had known she would be there, but she hadn't expected to look so damned silly when they first met.

Marty was talented, for sure, but she was also hot, and had a smattering of freckles right above her breasts. It had always been Helen's fantasy to connect the dots, one way or another. With that thought, Helen felt two light strokes on her legs and a quick wipe around the inside perimeter of her skirt. Oh, heart be still. The skirt relaxed.

"There you go." Marty raised herself to Helen's height and flung the towel onto the bar. She smiled broadly and her blue eyes danced appraisingly over Helen.

Stacey handed Marty her drink. "I think you have to marry her now."

"You're Helen Townsend," she said cheerfully. "I'm an avid reader of your column. I'm Marty Jamison." They shook hands.

"I admire your work, too," Helen said, having recovered her composure. "And thanks for rescuing me."

"My pleasure." Marty nudged Helen playfully. "You have the most fascinating mouth." Her eyes lowered to Helen's lips. "A cute little pout if you aren't smiling. Very kissable."

Helen blushed.

To the background music of Judy Garland at Carnegie

Hall, the guests arrived in small groups. Helen mingled and, much to her surprise, felt comfortable in the presence of many of the entertainment elite and their image-makers.

"Good God. That bitch is here," film director Jay Patton ranted to his lover. They dashed to the back of the room and wedged themselves between two ficus trees. Helen looked toward the bar as Blair Whitman ordered Scotch and rocks.

Helen knew the story. Blair was a temperamental hard-ass. Directors hated her, costars wanted to lock her into her trailer, and special effects crews thought seriously about blowing her to bits. Bam! Splat! Cut! Print it! And the cast could call it a wrap.

Blair had power and abused it to the hilt, but box office dollars had piled to mountainous proportions for her last three films and made nearly everyone connected to her work wealthy. She had Hollywood by their sensitive parts and she knew it. People sucked up to Blair Whitman.

"Well." Blair sidled up to Helen. "Meet the press." She took a long drink from her glass and her eyes narrowed. "Are we the next anecdote for your column, Ms. Townsend?"

"I failed Gossip one-oh-one," Helen said and scanned the room to see if Cory had arrived. "That's not why I'm here."

"People like you make me nervous." Blair walked a slow half circle around Helen as though sniffing her prey and readying to devour her.

"I'm not holding you hostage. You're free to leave," she said calmly, knowing that Blair was capable of going off the deep end when feeling threatened.

Marty walked over. "Cut it out, Blair."

The others watched in silence. Helen's eyes followed the arc that Blair walked. "Why are you afraid of me?" she asked.

Blair stopped abruptly, her brown hair jerked about her

shoulders. "I don't want a Michael Jackson done to me," she said with a chill to her voice.

The heavy smell of Scotch caused Helen to take a step back, and she raised her hand slightly to keep Stacey from coming closer.

"Then act like an adult," Helen said as the front door swung open and Cory walked in. Among snickers and cheers, Helen left Blair standing red-faced, apparently stunned with the remark. "Hey, baby." She kissed Cory and glanced at the woman that had arrived with her.

"Hello," the much too attractive Japanese woman said to Helen.

"Who's your friend?" Helen asked.

"Kim Lee. She's a cellist from the Philharmonic. Kim"— she slipped her arm around Helen's waist—"this is Helen."

"Hello." Kim smiled. "It isn't any wonder why Cory cut off Reinhardt's balls tonight." Without explanation of her comment, Kim joined Marty at the bar.

"Care to dance with me, Ms. Townsend?" Cory asked.

"I would." Helen led her to a less crowded area of the room and pulled her close. She moved her hands gently against the back of Cory's corduroy jacket. "So tell me about the castration."

"Reinhardt, the conductor, called me a pompous nobody. He kept stopping us, saying I was sloppy and not paying attention to his direction. After the sixth time, the entire orchestra was angry enough that I told him I had a date waiting and he could find himself a lesser-known nobody for Friday's concert, if he liked."

Helen was astounded. "You didn't say that." Cory nodded. "What did he say?"

"I would never play for an audience again." Cory

emphasized the end of the sentence with a quick nod to her head.

"Does he have that much power?"

"No. He's the pompous nobody. I left the building and I'll have an apology from him on my answering machine before morning."

Helen ran her hands through Cory's hair. "You did that for me?"

"Especially for you." She touched her fingertips to Helen's lips.

Helen felt a tapping on her shoulder. "I gotta steal your woman, Chambermaid." Stacey wedged herself between them.

Cory relinquished her hold on Helen and joined Kim in front of Warhol's *Marilyn Monroe*. Stacey began a pep talk, but Helen wasn't listening. She watched them, their heads together. Cory pulled something out of her pocket and flashed it. Kim's eyes widened when she looked closer at the object and then she hugged Cory. Cory seemed to enjoy their embrace and hugged Kim with as much enthusiasm.

Helen didn't like it or the feeling of jealousy that it provoked. Jealousy, a wasted emotion, as useful as rice in a drought.

"Are you ready?" Stacey asked. "Hey! Yoo-hoo!"

Helen snapped to attention. "What? I'm sorry, Stacey. What were you saying?"

"I said it's time you made your pitch to my pals."

Helen watched Cory place the object back into her pocket and Kim hugged her again. "I'm ready," she said.

"Let me get their attention. Good luck, Blondie." Stacey turned down the music, hopped up onto the bar, and was the voice of command. "Okay, ladies and gentlemen, although

I'm not sure who is what in this crowd." Laughter sprang from different directions, and pillows flew at her from all corners of the room. She motioned for Helen to join her. "You've met Helen and now she wants your undivided attention."

"I'm not standing on the bar," Helen said.

"You gotta in this crowd." Stacey grabbed her hands when several people hoisted Helen onto the bar. "Some of these heads are so big you can't see over them. Eye contact. Gotta have it."

"I'll sit on it, then."

Helen dangled her legs over the side of the bar and Stacey hopped down behind her. Helen surveyed the room for a moment and was impressed with the amount of talent before her. She could admit to herself that she was a bit starstruck, though she was able to hide most of her blind adoration.

There it was in front of her, the cream of the entertainment industry, flopped onto sofas and chairs, comfortable on the floor among the pillows. All eyes were on Helen. Actors, actresses, directors, producers, musicians, dancers. The list of big names in front of her was as impressive as the list of international cities that hung on Cory's walls. Even more impressive than the Queen.

"I feel insignificant in front of you," she said. "All of this talent. I want autographs later."

"What's up, Helen?" Mark Corrigan asked.

Helen hadn't prepared a speech. She wanted to feel her way in, would find her opening, and Mark became her target. His talk show had been rated number one for the past two years and Helen taped the show occasionally.

"Mark, I caught your show on lesbian and gay writers. What type of reaction did the show provoke?"

"Surprise. Most people didn't realize that big publishing houses don't like to touch these writers because of gay characters. In spite of the author's orientation, the audience was supportive."

"'Supportive in spite of their orientation,'" Helen said and gave her own spectators time to ponder the words. "I'm not a part of your world, but there is one thing that binds us and that's our sexuality." She paused. "You're the elite of this country. No matter what the papers report about you, no matter what you do or don't do, this country buys your product. The respect you command is second to none and I want you to lend out that respect."

"What are you saying, Helen?" Marty asked from the back of the crowd.

"This group has the resources to possibly make a significant difference in the attitudes of the straight world. You can lend a new dignity to the way the public perceives our population."

Blair laughed sarcastically. "And how do you propose we do that? Come out?" She walked closer. "Do you think we're crazy?" She slapped her empty glass onto the bar next to Helen. "Scotch," she demanded and eyeballed Helen without seeing Stacey pour ginger ale into the glass.

"Come out, yes. Crazy, no. Well, maybe crazy," she said with a smile. "I think talent borders on madness. We need more names out there. Every so often, there's a kiss-my-ass flurry of pride. Ellen, Melissa—"

"Mark Corrigan!" Nick yelled.

Mark grinned and dug his hands into the pockets of his Levi's. "I don't want my head bashed in."

Helen countered. "You're like wolves; you travel in packs. There's a great deal of protection there."

"Lost work," said costume designer Jenny Colgate.

"Jenny, you won an Oscar last year for *Devil's Rain*. Producers will continue to buy that talent."

"I agree with Jenny," Nick answered.

"Nick, look at your gorgeous face," Helen teased him. "You've been the number one box office draw for the last five years. Look at these people." She waved her arm over the room. "They produce and direct you. I doubt they'll stop because you come out. You have the power. The Moral Majority may sound off for a while, but it all comes flying back to the almighty dollar."

"You're right," one of the producers said, "but the family matter is a different thing. Not all of us are out to them."

"That's a priority I can understand. If you aren't out to them, I wouldn't expect you to consider my request."

Blair took a swig of her fresh drink, choked on the unexpected blast of sugar, and glared at Stacey. She looked back at Helen. "Can you understand this? We can't change the world. They aren't ready for us."

Helen looked at her and winked playfully, much to Blair's disdain. "Perhaps more people are than we're aware of."

"There've been marches," Cory chimed in.

"Been there," Jay said.

"Done that. Got the T-shirt." Jenny flopped onto the sofa beside him.

Helen answered the group. "This won't be a picket sign, march-around-the-Capitol thing. I'm talking about a class act, using your combined talents."

"What exactly do you propose?" Marty asked.

Helen leaned back onto her palms and took a deep breath. "This will sound like nearly every Andy Hardy film ever made, but I think you should combine your talents in a night of knock-'em-dead entertainment. The difference from Andy Hardy is at the end, when you come out as a group." Murmurs filled the room. "From the master of ceremonies to every act, the show will be empowered by gays and lesbians."

"You're nuts," Blair said. "And how do you figure in with this grand display of yours? Hide behind your column and write about it afterward? How incredibly brave of you, Ms. Townsend. We risk our necks so you and Chamberlain can hold hands in public."

Blair's sarcasm brought a quick reaction from Cory. With a snap of her arm she shoved her bottle of spring water into Kim's hand and quickly approached Blair who stood with a smile.

"Watch your words, Blair," Cory said, her face inches away from Blair's. "I won't permit anyone to speak to Helen like that."

Helen smiled to herself as she listened to the exchange. Protection? Possessiveness? Territorial boundaries not to be trespassed upon, and especially by the likes of Blair? Helen looked over to where Kim stood—still smiling. Maybe Helen should set up a few boundaries of her own.

Don't cross my line, Kim who plays a cello. I trust the Japanese with my electronics but not with my woman.

"Come off it, Chamberlain," Blair said. "Do you have to be so damn honorable?"

"Honorable is better than inebriated, and it's because of your inebriation that I won't ask you to apologize to Helen." Cory quieted. "Now…" She reached up and straightened Blair's collar. "Listen to Helen or don't. Just keep your pretty lips shut." She returned to her place beside Kim.

Blair was appalled. "Stacey, are you going to allow her to talk to me like that? Can't you put a leash—" She was mortified when Stacey grabbed her by the arm, led her to a sofa, and pushed her down with a heavy hand.

"Yes, I can. Stop being a pain in the ass, Blair." Stacey sat beside her and nodded for Helen to continue.

Helen answered Blair. "I want to be there, as MC for the evening. I'm not the talent showcase. That will be provided by all of you."

Marty joined Helen and placed her hand on her leg. She turned to the group. "I want to do it. Let's shake 'em up a little."

"Someone's already shaken Helen too much. Her brain's loosened up," Blair said.

Cory started for Blair but stopped when Stacey grabbed Blair's arm. Stacey warned her. "You've got nothing on me, you little actress. I won't think twice about sending you out the door."

Blair seethed with anger and humiliation. She glared at Stacey and pushed herself from the sofa. "I don't have to take this abuse. Get my coat," she demanded of her hostess.

"Get it yourself," Stacey said and joined the women at the bar. Blair stormed to the closet and pulled her coat on. "Good night, Blair."

Blair pointed to Helen. "Don't let her fuck up your lives," she said to the room and then pointed to Stacey. "I'll talk to *you* later." She slammed the door behind her.

Except for Judy torching "Stormy Weather," the room was quiet, and when Stacey brushed against Helen's arm, Helen jumped.

"Turn up the volume, Jenny. Come on, guys, relax," Stacey said to her guests.

"So that's Blair Whitman. Whew!" Helen pretended to wipe her brow.

"That was nothing, sweetheart," Marty said and grabbed a celery stick from the bar. "She behaved rather well."

Cory still watched the door. "Why did she act like a wounded puppy when you—"

"I've never seen her react to anyone like that," Marty said to Helen.

Stacey grinned. "I'll pay for it. Blair and I, well, we've been…sort of, uh…seeing each other for the past month."

"What?" Marty said.

"Nothing serious. You know me. We're just dating," she said and poured herself another glass of wine.

"We do know you," Marty said. "You're dating her brains out."

With Blair out of the way, Helen mingled and found that everyone was at least talking about her idea. There was an air of skepticism combined with an equal amount of enthusiasm.

"Give it some thought," she said to them. "Just let me know in a few weeks."

Helen joined Cory, who was again closerthanthis to Kim. Stacey ousted Judy's album and replaced her with Doris Day. What would be, would be.

"It's an interesting idea," Kim said. "I'll think about it, and I'd like to have your number."

"Of course. Before we leave." She turned to Cory. "Let's finish our dance."

"I think you'll win some over," Cory said. "Artists love power, and you've just offered us the world."

Cory placed her hands near Helen's throat. Helen enjoyed the soft stroke of fingers that brushed her neck. It was Cory's favorite resting place for fingers and her lips.

"Helen," Cory said, "there's something you need to know."

Helen's stomach knotted.

Damn it. She seldom called her Helen unless it was serious. And that damn Kim still watched them and smiled. Fine. Tell me you and Kim are seeing each other. Tell me you need your space. Just go ahead and shred my heart to pieces, right here in front of Marty and Jenny and Jay and Stacey. Damn it all. I'm falling in love with you. Don't you know that?

"Why doesn't she take her flawless face right the hell out of here?" Helen grumbled loudly.

Cory took a step back. "Excuse me?"

"Kim." Helen narrowed her eyes toward Kim and then she looked at Cory. "Is she what you have to tell me about?"

"You think Kim and I—"

"I understand you may see other women—"

"Really?"

"—but you could have chosen a better time."

Cory grabbed Helen's belt buckle and yanked her closer. "What kind of a person do you think I am?"

"Ambushes are in your blood. How pompous you must feel having both of—"

"Both of who?"

"Well, look at the two of you. All night. Smiles and giggles."

"You don't know what you're talking about."

"You don't know what I'm feeling."

"It's perfectly clear, Helen. You're jealous."

"It's not like I've put a ring on your finger, but—"

"I see." Cory's expression softened. "Would you like the bottom line?"

"The very bottom line, and don't look so smug."

"Okay." She looked into Helen's eyes and with her fingertips drew a line from Helen's chin to the back of her neck. Helen tried not to weaken from her look and her touch, but the situation was hopeless. "I'm Delphinus," she said.

Helen remembered the constellation and leaned her cheek into Cory's warm palm. "What's that supposed to mean?" she asked with all of the weakness that the touch had provoked.

"I want you to take another look, Helen. Look deeper, beyond the surface. You'll find where I am with you."

Helen searched the eyes that she hadn't resisted from day one, that she couldn't resist tonight, and that she knew she wouldn't resist thirty years from now. That she was sure of. She was also sure that Cory was the most important part of her life. Helen looked long into those eyes and soon caught her own reflection, the reflection of a woman in love. That's what Helen found.

Cory pulled Helen slowly against her. Her arms wrapped tightly around her, and Helen melted into them. Helen kissed Cory's neck, her ear. She nuzzled into her silky hair, wanting her, not wanting to share her.

She's yours, Helen. Tell her.

"I love you," Helen whispered into Cory's ear.

Cory murmured a soft sound of joy and held Helen tighter. "I love you, too." She brushed her thumb across Helen's lips and replaced it with her mouth. Their kiss was gentle and finalized their words. Cory moved back slightly. "It's early for us, but in the future we might decide to be together permanently. We can't be married in New York, but if we could, I'd be sure to ask you."

Helen liked the thought. She cocked her head. "Ask me now."

"Maybe someday you'll marry me? Would you be my bride?"

Having Cory to love and to feel loved by her presented an irresistible package for Helen. But there was one matter that, if they couldn't agree upon it, could change the course of their relationship immediately.

"One of the first things you knew about me is that I want out of the closet," she said and Cory nodded. "Living together is a statement without much danger. Boasting about it to an auditorium full of people, however, could prove hazardous to our careers and to our lives. If we're together, I need you on stage with me or we won't work."

"I'm proud to love you. I'll be with you that night."

Helen took Cory's hands into hers, pulled her close, and held tightly. At the very least, they could exchange rings with private vows. Maybe invite some friends and maybe not. They could legally take the other's name. Helen Townsend-Chamberlain. She liked the hyphen.

"Yes, baby," she said in answer to Cory's proposal. "The odds are in your favor." As an afterthought she joked, "Do I get a pre-engagement ring?"

"I had something a bit different in mind. Close your eyes." Helen closed her eyes and felt Cory's fingers place something around her neck, and then she turned her around. "Now open them."

She'd been strategically danced to a mirror. In the reflection dangled a delicate gold chain around her neck with a stunning pear-shaped emerald. It rested gracefully below her throat as if cultured specifically to lie there.

Tears came to Helen's eyes. "It's beautiful," she said and ran her fingers along the chain. It was Helen's bottle of Midori, the same chromatic essence that became Cory. She turned back to her. "Absolutely perfect."

"Yes." Cory gathered the stone into her hand. "It took a while to find the right stone."

"No, I mean you." Helen slipped a ring from her hand. An opal was surrounded by tiny pearls. It had belonged to her great-grandmother, Emily Townsend. Helen placed it on Cory's left hand. "Now it's complete."

Cory twisted the ring back and forth. Fiery orange and fluorescent green came alive. She'd always admired the ring, had often toyed with it during their hours of snuggle-talk, and she knew the ring was an heirloom.

"Are you sure you want to let it out of the family?"

"You're my family now, baby. You're my future."

CHAPTER THIRTEEN

If nothing came of Helen's proposed cavalcade of stars, at least she'd made friends with Marty. They were almost inseparable when Cory was away. Shopping, dining, and even an occasional night of just two girls sitting around and shooting the bull over cocktails. Marty was fun, but brutal with her exercise, especially when she needed to burn some calories.

In Marty's living room, Helen dropped to the floor, exhausted from their tyrannical workout. She panted and coughed. Her hair was plastered to the sides of her face. Sweat streamed down her back, between her breasts, down the back of her shorts. Vast wet spots soaked her underarms. She wiped her face with a towel, coughed again, and stared at the hardwood floor. Marty stretched onto her back and continued with cool-down exercises.

It took all her remaining energy for Helen to ask the big question. "Are we sweating or glistening?"

Marty laughed. "We smell like the Bronx Zoo. My guess is sweating."

"Thanks," she mumbled and watched Marty, who was obviously not sharing Helen's near-death experience. "How can you do this day after day?"

"It's my life, sweetheart." She lifted both knees from the

floor toward her chin, lowered them, and repeated the exercise several times. "Gotta do it to dance." She stopped and took a deep breath. "What do writers do to keep their fingers in shape?" She made crawly spider motions with her hands.

"Hell, I still don't know how to type." Helen wiped her face again. "My eyes dart around that keyboard like I'm watching a miniature tennis match."

"Really? Tiny Martinas and Gabriellas battling from A to L. Come on." She grunted, pushed herself up, and yanked Helen to her feet. "Let's get some fluids back into us."

Helen plopped onto the kitchen chair and chugged her glass of orange-pineapple juice. She then dangled her arms, resigned to exhaustion. "Just shoot me now." She wiped her mouth with her sleeve. "I must have a death wish. I've been doing this for three weeks with you. This isn't a friendship. This is cruel and unusual punishment."

"You'll live. Besides, we need you." Marty took a Salem from the pack on the table, lit it, and inhaled deeply. "Do you mind?" she asked and blew out the smoke.

"No. What do you mean? Who needs me?"

She dragged again. "People listen when you talk. Do you realize that?"

"Well, yes, otherwise I wouldn't have a column. What people are you referring to?"

"The gang. Us. That group of dummies you sliced your wrists for. We're selling our souls for you, sweetheart. Hasn't anyone called you?"

"No," she said, dumbfounded from the sudden news.

"It figures. They think everybody can read their minds. Stardom does it." Marty scratched vigorously at her scalp. "I need a shower."

"I can see that. Now tell me what's going on!"

Marty tapped ashes into the ashtray. "We figured you would take care of all that."

Helen threw her arms into the air. "All of what? I didn't even know—" The phone rang. "I'll be right back."

"I don't believe this," Helen said with disgust to the empty kitchen. Then she sighed. "I seem to spend a lot of time lately talking to empty rooms or condiments. Or myself."

Marty returned, in a flurry of excitement. "I have to run out." She shoved a towel and facecloth into Helen's hand. "Grab a shower. I'll be back soon."

"Marty!"

"Later," she said while trotting down the hallway. The front door slammed shut.

Helen found the bathroom, stripped, and studied her body in a mirrored wall. Sideways, definitely her favorite angle because she couldn't see the width of her hips, which weren't so bad except in her own mind. Her breasts were still firm and her thighs were holding up well.

A light birthmark, the shape of a quarter rest, near the top of her right thigh reminded her that Cory would return from Atlanta tomorrow. She touched the mark and smiled. Cory often rested there. Helen missed her with her constant traveling, but if the symphony decided to accept her as maestro, she would settle in or around Boston and then they would deal with how to be together. At least she wouldn't be gallivanting all over the world.

During her shower, Helen remembered one of the many discussions they'd had concerning Cory's relocation.

One particular conversation had taken place in the music room, when Helen had quietly opened the door and carried a tray inside. Cory, who was deep into practice, had been at the piano for two hours and Helen had decided it was time to break.

Cory's nose suddenly twitched. She raised her head to the aroma of fresh-baked bread. She continued playing but the delicious smell grew stronger, too strong to blow off as the neighbor's air escaping into her apartment. Helen knew what Cory was thinking: Had her Helen, her non-cooking, potato-nuking Helen, actually broken out the flour and eggs? Helen carried the lip-smacking, mouthwatering snack closer. Cory stopped playing, turned, and her eyes lit up like the Christmas tree at Rockefeller Plaza.

"Yes!" She squealed when she saw a tray that bore freshly baked bread tucked snugly into a wicker basket. Fresh orange slices nestled with kiwi and buttery morsels of Swiss and Cheddar cheese.

Helen remained straight-faced. "Yoko dropped this off," she said, and Cory smiled. "She said to fatten you up." Helen placed the tray on the back of the grand piano and Cory followed.

"Did Yoko send any messages?" Cory asked nonchalantly and then tore into the steamy loaf.

"Yes." Helen thought. "Something about a walrus and an egg man." She watched Cory struggle to control a laugh. "And then she pointed to the kiwi and said 'Give these a chance.' What do you suppose it means?"

Cory sighed, nodded, and fed Helen a creamy chunk of Swiss cheese. "The first part is top secret, but the second part"—she swept her eyes over Helen's face—"means you have flour all over your pretty little cheeks."

Helen looked at her reflection on the piano and saw nearly enough flour to make a small pretzel. "Before Yoko left she yanked a huge powder-puff out of her sleeve and slammed it into my face." She brushed off the flour with a napkin. "It was the strangest thing. She likes slapstick, is my guess."

Cory was beside herself with laughter. She raised her finger to the air in emphasis. "Ah, yes. That's Yoko's 'You gotta move to Boston' powder-puff slamming."

"You'll have to relocate," Helen said.

Cory munched an orange slice. "I wouldn't mind supporting you if you wanted to get back to your book."

"I love you, but I'm not so sure I want to move to Boston. My life is here."

"You could change that."

"So could you. Stay in New York."

And so it would go each time.

Rejuvenated by a cool shower and donning fresh clothes, Helen wrapped a towel around her hair. In her search for Marty, she checked the living room and kitchen, but Marty was nowhere in sight. Back down the hallway, she headed toward an open door and peeked into a bedroom.

"Marty?" No answer.

A throat cleared in the dead air and Helen turned toward the muffled sound. Another sound, lighter and less masculine followed. A woman's giggle, a muffled "ouch" and a "shh" led her to another door, and the distinct clamoring inside stopped Helen. She listened, curious.

"Face the door," someone whispered. "She'll—" Ping! Many giggles then, when someone hit what sounded like a very high piano key. "Shh!" the same voice said. "You're worse than children."

"I don't know the words," someone whispered desperately.

"What? Everybody knows—" The voice was cut off by a chorus of "Shh!"

Helen chuckled. Somewhere in that disorganized mess, Marty could probably be found. She turned the door handle.

"Marty?"

"Yeah, come on in, Helen."

"The door's locked."

More laughter echoed from inside.

"Shit." Footsteps pounded on the hardwood floor, the door swung open, and Marty grabbed Helen's hand and pulled her inside. "Ta da! Hit it, Chamberlain."

Helen was surprised not only to see Cory home a day early but also to find almost everybody from the party there, as well as some who hadn't been there, like Jackie Payne, a sleek, soft-butch makeup artist. Blair, she noticed, was absent, and she supposed that was just as well.

They sang together, "When You Wish Upon A Star." Some sounded good, some off-key, and some struggled through their laughter. Cory removed one hand from the piano keys long enough to blow her a kiss. Helen listened while they sang, and she half expected to see Jiminy Cricket dance across the room in his tuxedo.

Helen had made her wish to the stars and it seemed that they would make it come true. Not only her wish, it was obviously their own secret longing, to honor themselves and those who were their equal. She couldn't believe that they'd agreed, and she wanted to hug each of them. The makings of a top-notch show were right there in front of her, and the thought of it gave her goose bumps.

"This is wonderful. We're really gonna do it." Helen punched the air in front of her. "Yeah!"

"It's your ball game, Helen. We give you the talent and you give us the ways and means," Mark said.

Her ball game. Suddenly she was launched into the role

of producer. That meant getting their acts together, locating a hall or theater, setting a show date, producing programs, and probably a million other things she knew absolutely nothing about. She'd probably rely on Marty for insider advice, but she couldn't wait to get started.

Cory left the piano and joined Helen.

"How did you keep this from me?" Helen asked after a long kiss from Cory and wolf whistles from the group.

"I—" She stopped abruptly as she looked toward the doorway.

Marty raised her eyebrows and a chorus of groans came from the others. Helen turned and looked behind her.

Blair leaned against the wall outside the door. She was squeezed into black spandex accessorized with a silver belt buckle, three-inch heels, and dark glasses. Her arms were folded in front of her. She looked sexy, something Helen would never admit to thinking, but Blair's cold demeanor gave true meaning to the term icy-hot.

"I couldn't resist crashing your little get-together." Her voice was cool and steady.

"You're welcome here any time," Marty said, walking to the door. "I didn't think you'd be interested—"

"Well, I am." She pushed away from the wall and walked into the room. "I have something to say about this Townsend Shock Appeal." She looked toward Cory. "It's my turn to speak." She paused for effect.

"Helen gets paid, rather hefty I presume, to stir up controversy." She walked slowly around Helen. "Like us, she's just another closeted queer." Cory stepped up to Blair. Blair stopped and turned quickly to Helen. "Does that word offend you?"

"Not in this group," Helen said.

Blair looked at Cory and smiled triumphantly. "Then I'll continue. This is one story Helen can't do alone, unlike Moses, who parted an entire sea."

"With Divine intervention," Jenny said. "And he was leading his people."

Blair laughed. "They packed up their worldly goods and followed, in search of the Promised Land. Their Bill of Rights, so to speak."

"What's your point, Blair?" Stacey asked.

"My point is that all of you, except for you, Stacey, could possibly throw away your livelihoods for this woman's personal need. There won't be Divine intervention and there's no promise at the end. There's only hope where hope isn't enough." She looked at Helen. "But it can't be left to lie and rot, can it, Helen? You need to wear that robe and carry that staff."

"I'm not Moses," Helen said. "Look. I don't—"

"No, you aren't a prophet and these people are mad to follow you. Your proposed show is the most absurd and foolish thing I've ever heard of and if you think I'd throw away everything I've earned, for the sake of freedom, freedom that I shouldn't have to fight for to begin with, then you're..." Blair paused and smiled. She removed her sunglasses and returned Helen's wink from the party "...absolutely correct."

The group around the piano let out their breath together and Cory did a double take on Blair.

Helen blinked, stunned by the words. "What?"

Blair responded with less bravura. "All of them can't be wrong, Helen. I've thought about this for weeks, and the worst that can happen is I won't work in Hollywood for a while. I could use a break, anyway."

"Crazy woman," Jay whispered.

"Am I in?" Blair asked. "I'd really like to do this show with you and I promise not to ask for top billing."

Helen blinked again and looked around the room. Except for Jay, all heads nodded approval. "You're in," she said quietly and began to laugh. "She's in."

"Oh, goody," Jay grumbled.

CHAPTER FOURTEEN

Helen sat in the stream of late morning sunlight. Her orange juice and rye toast remained untouched. Her hair was a tangled mess, Medusa-like. Helen Townsend just wasn't glamorous in the mornings, and she didn't care.

Her definition of breakfast couldn't be found in any dictionary. Breakfast meant: "Leave me alone while I have coffee and toast. Don't expect me to talk until I'm showered. Confine your cereal to the bowl and please clean up the mess. I am not your mother or your nanny. I am not human. I'm a lump. Treat me as such."

Cory, on the other hand, sat wide-awake, her nose buried in the pages of the newspaper, oblivious to the sounds of her breakfast cereal. Snap-crackle-pop. Snap-crackle-pop. Snap-crackle-pop. Every morning Cory was home, Helen heard it. Snap-crackle-pop. The continuous battering of sound was grating.

"Says here that Webber's fired Dunaway from *Sunset Boulevard*," Cory said of the Broadway musical. She dunked her spoon into the bowl, and a heap of cereal fell over the side. Snap-crackle-pop. "Probably blown out of proportion by the press." The loaded spoon disappeared past Cory's lips and emerged again, empty.

Helen raised an eyebrow and grumbled a word. "Meaning?"

"Sensationalism." She splashed into the bowl with her spoon. Cereal scattered onto the table.

"Is that how you see my profession?" Helen asked, an edge to her voice.

"Not always." She dunked the spoon again. Whoosh went the cereal. "But you do hype stories."

Helen counted twenty-seven bits of toasted rice that were scattered about the table, to her annoyance, while Cory chatted endlessly and looked disgustingly well groomed for that hour of the day. Well groomed, but sloppy in her eating habits. Helen wished Cory was as careful at her own breakfast table as she was in a public restaurant. Cory turned the page of her paper and her hand knocked the bowl.

"I know a woman," Helen said calmly and got up. "She worked with me on fiction." She walked to the cabinet. "She got me so crazy that I called her a word-sucking vampire." She pulled a large crystal salad bowl from the cabinet and slammed it onto the counter. "She told me the characters needed conflict."

"Uh-huh." Cory's nose remained in the paper.

With fluid motion, Helen dragged the bowl from the counter, reached up, snatched a ladle from above the butcher block, dropped it into the oversized bowl, and stopped beside Cory. She banged the bowl onto the table. Cory jumped.

"I wish I'd known you then," Helen said.

Cory looked puzzled. "Is there a problem?"

Helen glared. "No. No problem." She grabbed Cory's cereal bowl with both hands, dumped its contents into the larger bowl, and slammed it back down on the table.

Cory folded the paper. She looked at the bowl and then at Helen. "What's the matter?"

Helen picked up the large bowl. "Hold this," she said and then scooped the spilled cereal into her palm and held it over the bowl. "This is the matter." She emptied the stray pieces into the bowl. "Every morning—dunk, splash, snap-crackle-pop. I've asked you lovingly and then politely. Now I'm telling you. No more snap-crackle-pop if I gotta clean up the mess."

"I wash my dishes," Cory said.

"This isn't about dirty dishes. Every morning you turn our breakfast table into chaos."

"Well, I'll alert the media: 'Chamberlain Gets Careless.'"

Helen stomped to the cabinet, grabbed the box of Rice Krispies, and trashed it. "I *am* the media, and you'll *get* shredded wheat."

"What is it with you? You complain if I'm not here and you complain when I am. Eat in the dining room if you're unhappy in here."

Helen stormed out of the kitchen, into her writing room, and slammed the door. She powered up her computer, popped a disk into the drive, and watched the flickering green light. She needed a moment to come down from her anger and pondered whether she should work, in her current state. If she started a column, she might sensationalize, bend the arrow.

"My readers eat it up and my lover criticizes me. Even weathermen get to exaggerate."

They don't merely say it snowed, they'll tell you how high, how long, how fast, how deadly. Gale force winds. Major storm blowing in. Major power outages. Major roadways impassable. Major this, major that, none of which should be confused with the Major Deegan Bridge, and that is, by the way, closed.

And now for local conditions.

Helen shut down the computer and headed for the door. She yanked it open.

"Al Roker from NBC wouldn't take that crap from you," she yelled toward the kitchen.

One. Two. Three. Helen counted the seconds before Cory charged down the hallway.

"You want to fight?" She pushed past Helen. "Look at this room. Reams of paper. Reference books. Piles of…*stuff* everywhere."

"It's my work and it's not in your way."

Cory picked up a silver lightning-bolt SS insignia from the desk. "This is work? Surrounding yourself with death? Look at the walls! You have more photographs than the Holocaust Museum. It's wallpaper, and badly hung. The Nazis had a better sense of organization than you have."

"Don't ever glorify those bastards to me."

"I want you to clean up the room." She picked up a small battered aluminum vial from the top of Helen's monitor. "Look." She wiped the dusty cap. "What is all of this junk?"

Helen grabbed the vial and shook it in Cory's face.

"A hair ribbon. My father opened an oven door and saw a little girl wearing two pink hair ribbons. The Nazis were less organized at that point."

She pulled a black-and-white photograph from a pile near the desk. Bodies filled a trench fifty feet long and twenty feet wide. She shoved the picture toward Cory's face.

"He was on detail to straighten out the dead for a decent burial." She grabbed a Luger from a leather holster. "A man, just bones, walked up to my father and asked him to shoot him. Dad refused but didn't take the gun away soon enough. The man blew his own brains out." She seized a stack of photographs and flung them against the wall. "That's what this junk is. He faced this horror. He took these pictures. He ate, slept, and lived death for two weeks."

She hurried into their bedroom and curled up with a pillow to hug away the hurt. She thought of her father as a young soldier, the revulsion he had faced while the camps were liberated. A hero to the survivors, he had felt more like a funeral director.

A few minutes later, she heard Cory enter the room. She found comfort with Cory curled against her. Cautiously, she slipped an arm around her waist.

"You never told me," Cory said. "I'm sorry."

"We talked about writing a book and then he died." Helen sobbed. "People still don't believe." She opened her eyes. "He wanted them to remember."

"You share his convictions."

"Not exactly. His convictions would just as soon see people like us shot, yet he despised Hitler for the deaths. I couldn't convince him that his homophobia was the same prejudice."

"It explains your passion to make the show happen. You want the world to see." She ran her fingers through Helen's hair. "You're a strong woman."

"Not so strong, maybe." Helen sat up, pulled a tissue from the box, and blew hard.

"Why do you say that?"

Helen wiped her eyes and blew again. She looked down at Cory. "There's another box of Rice Krispies in the cabinet."

"I know."

Helen stared at Cory. She loved her hair, thought it beautiful, but was dying to get her hands on it. A cut, just to the shoulders, would transform Cory into a new beauty. Short bangs that could fly all over, if she liked. It seemed their way.

"You have that look in your eyes again." Cory moved

from the bed and held her index fingers up to form a cross. "Stay away from my hair."

"Aw, please. Just to your shoulders. It'll be a whole new look for you."

"I like my French braid."

"It'll be long enough. Come on, baby. Let me cut your hair."

"No!" Cory turned away and scooted down the hall, chased by the lunatic with the scissors. "Go away!" She laughed when cornered against a porcelain Apollo.

"Do it for me. Your audience will love it."

"I didn't realize I wasn't attractive enough for you." Cory half-smiled.

"You are, but—"

"Then my hair is fine just as it is. End of subject."

Cory won this time, but Helen was determined to get her one way or another. In her sleep, maybe. No, she might be a Samson, and Helen would hate to take her talent away. Then again, it would put an end to the Boston conversations. She smiled mischievously and released her prisoner.

You're terrible.

CHAPTER FIFTEEN

Given Cory's status of lover in absentia, telephone conversations filled Helen's evening hours. Marty, Blair, Jenny, and Kim—who probably continued to smile, even over the phone. The troupe was as excited as she was for what some of them called "the performance of their lifetime."

There was also plenty of time for the multitude of tasks that fell to her as producer. The toughest was booking a theater or auditorium. Frustrated enough at one point, she would have fought the hookers for territory off Forty-Second Street provided the lighting was sufficient and refreshments were made available for intermission.

Off-Broadway was impossible. Shows were in constant changeover, with one lot of performers being herded out while the next was herded in, leaving no open stage. Marty explained that stage time was so precious that critics were often paid to write negative reviews that would close down a show. True? Helen didn't know or really care. All that mattered was finding space for their night.

Where would they go? Jersey? Connecticut? Helen thought not. They'd stay in New York. Broadway. Those were the true stages. Right. If her name was Gerald Schoenfeld, the chairman for the Shubert Organization—which probably owned half of the theaters in New York—she'd ace an auditorium in seconds. How could she dare to hope for space for even a single night with nothing but an MA in journalism?

Blair had suggested Hollywood, and Helen almost considered the idea, but had said no. It felt too commercial when she wanted nonprofit.

Pay dirt. After three weeks of relentless hounding, not to mention a little help from Marty, who had cashed in on some favors, Helen received a call from the Stanwyck Theater.

"We have one day open and that's March the sixth. The theater is also available that morning for rehearsals. You've a persistent friend," the manager said. "Ms. Jamison refused to take no for an answer. There is one last thing, Ms. Townsend—the fee."

She narrowed her eyes, expecting to hear big money. "Yes?"

"The fee is waived. The box office is yours." He sighed.

She sighed stronger, in relief. "Thank you very much." She flipped her pencil through the air and slammed the phone down. Piece of cake.

❖

For the remainder of the evening, Helen took off her producer's hat. After a hot shower, she snuggled onto the sofa and watched her favorite movie once more. *Love Story.*

"*I don't want Paris,*" the dying Jenny said to Oliver.

Helen, a sucker for the pain and Jenny's devotion to Oliver in the midst of dying, dabbed her eyes.

"It's you she wants, Oliver. Not Paris," Helen said to the screen.

"And I want time," Jenny said, *"which you can't give me."*

Before she could slip into her old "poor Helen and Chelsea" mode, the phone rang and she answered in the middle of the second ring.

"Were you waiting that close to the phone?" Cory asked.

"Uh-huh," she said, and lowered the volume of the television. "You're always prompt. I want every second."

"My cameo appearances are frustrating for me as well."

"Are you in Cleveland?"

"Yes, of all places, but I always have a terrific audience here."

"It sounds wonderful. It means you'll be home soon." Helen hugged her pillow.

"Uh, maybe not."

Helen's heart sank. "Why not?"

"Liz called. Kirk Janssen wants me to stand in for him Friday."

Silence.

"You're never home," Helen whined.

"I didn't give an answer," Cory said to the unasked question. "I told her I would have to discuss it with you."

"Come home. End of discussion."

Cory let out a long breath. "It's a wonderful opportunity for me."

"So when's our opportunity?" Helen asked and received no answer. "When will you be home?"

"Saturday afternoon, but I thought maybe you could fly up on Friday, hear the concert, and we could spend the weekend in Boston. It would be our first time together in another city."

"Is this another get-Helen-to-Boston ploy?"

"No. It's an idea. I miss you."

With those magic words, Helen perked up. "It's a wonderful idea. I'll hop a flight from Kennedy Airport."

"Great. My flight arrives at two, so try to work around that time. I'll let you know where I'm staying, in case we get our wires crossed."

"Okay, baby. Hey, I'm proud of you, Cory Chamberlain."

Not long after she reserved a flight to Logan Airport, Helen received another phone call. It had to be Cory at that hour, something she may have forgotten to mention earlier.

"Hey, baby," Helen said seductively.

"Hello, darling," a voice whispered deliciously.

Helen was wide-eyed. Cory never called her darling. The whisper was familiar, but she couldn't place it.

"Who is this?"

The voice whispered, "One of your Israelites."

Helen thought. "Ah. Then may I call you Michael? Or would you prefer Mr. Jackson?"

"You're a snot, Townsend."

"Me?" She laughed. "What's that song Jackson recorded about starting with the man in the mirror?"

"Okay, I get your drift. Listen, I'm flying to Boston Friday afternoon. Do you want to have lunch with me beforehand?"

"Really? I'm booked for Boston, too. That's a strange coincidence. I wonder what the odds are—"

"Slim to none, and stop making it sound so creepy. My departure is three thirty."

Helen raised her eyebrows. "Mine, too. Wow."

"Knock it off, Helen."

"Sorry. Yeah, let's have lunch first. How about meeting me at the paper, say noon?"

"Fine. By the way, there's a matter you need to address. I think I'm about to throw a wrench into your queer show."

"How's that?"

"I was watching the news tonight. The dock workers are on strike in Oakland, California."

Like she cared. "What does that have to do with us?"

"Does the word 'union' mean anything to you?"

"Of course it does. Unions protect just about any worker in the United States."

"Like actors? Wardrobe? Makeup?"

"Among others." When a mental list of those she knew belonged to an organization, and those who had never worked in the theater, flashed through her mind, she sat upright. "Oh, shit. Some of us need union cards."

"You catch on quickly, Ms. Townsend."

"I need to call everyone immediately." Another fifteen phone calls before she could call it a night didn't thrill her.

Blair laughed. "You sound like your palms are sweaty and your heart's racing."

"Yeah, a shock wave of 'what the hell am I doing?' just tore through me."

"Well, relax. Anyone involved knows they need the proper credentials. I just wanted to spook you."

Helen's tense muscles relaxed, but now she was pissed off. "You really are a bitch."

Still, she laughed. "I wish I could have seen your expression. Are we still on for tomorrow?"

"I guess so, but you're buying lunch and the cab. Good night, Blair."

"Wait. There's one more matter."

"You better make it worth my time," Helen said.

"You may not call me Michael."

Chapter Sixteen

A fax came over Helen's office machine. Cory had sent a rundown of her Friday night program. They would open with Mozart's "The Marriage of Figaro Overture," a fabulous opening with great power. Helen knew Cory was tickled. Then would come Bach's "Air On the G String." Couldn't he have come up with a classier title? Either way, the piece possessed the ability to lull Helen to sleep. The next one was underlined, with a happy face drawn next to it. Chopin's "Military Polonaise." Helen cringed. That music Cory had practiced repeatedly, ad nauseam, and Helen had learned to loathe the piece.

The list continued. Wagner's "Ride of the Valkyries," works by Bizet, Chabrier, Tchaikovsky, and Sousa. Then Copland's "Simple Gifts," followed by the last piece, Anderson's "Sleigh Ride." A great night for music. "I love you," the fax ended.

A house gopher poked his head into Helen's office.

"Helen, some woman on line seven says she's Michael Jackson."

"Thanks." She grabbed the phone and punched in the line. "Hello, Mikey."

"Our flight's been canceled."

"Don't bullshit me, Blair. I wanted to smack you last night."

"No fooling. I called to confirm. There's a mechanical problem, but we're on a flight at eight."

Helen pouted. Cheated again. She wanted to see Cory at five, not wait until ten and miss the concert as well as the extra time with her. She appreciated the classics as well as the next person and she'd never heard the Boston Light Orchestra live. She would miss the fun.

"What a bunch of bull," Helen said.

"Griping won't get us there any sooner. We can't drive. We'll hit every imaginable traffic pocket. An early dinner for us instead of lunch, then?"

"New York Deli at four," Helen said.

At least she'd have a great Reuben.

❖

Inside the flight terminal, Helen removed her coat, but Blair remained dressed. She'd included dark glasses and a wide-brimmed floppy hat to conceal her identity.

"Can't disturb the natives," she said and pulled the brim lower to her eyes.

Helen looked up from her boarding pass. A smiling, black-vested, male flight attendant approached their seats.

"Miss Whitman and Miss Townsend?" he asked.

"Yes," Helen said.

"The captain has asked me to seat you before the normal rush. I'll take your passes, and you can follow me, please."

"Great," Blair said and leaned toward Helen. "It's good to be the king."

They entered the narrow ramp to Flight 1201, and the attendant stopped at the third row of first class seats.

"I'll take the window seat," Blair said and shoved her hat into the overhead compartment.

With the aisle on her right, Helen got comfy in her seat and pulled her lap belt across and buckled it. When she noticed Blair's was still at her side, she picked it up and handed it to her.

"Kings of Pop wear them, too," she said.

Blair took the belt and snapped it into position. "You know, if this plane goes down, that belt won't do jack for me."

"And if you don't wear it, you'll be thrown off the flight, and I'm not going with you. Isn't it grand that life offers choices?" Helen smiled at Blair's kiss-my-ass expression.

The flurry of boarding passengers grew louder, and soon the attendants instructed the standard lifesaving techniques. The captain welcomed his passengers and announced they were cleared for takeoff. All passengers were instructed to remain in their seats, belts fastened, and please observe the no smoking regulation.

Minutes afterward, thundering engines increased power and hurtled the aircraft down the runway. Blair grabbed a firm hold of Helen's hand. "Do you mind? Takeoff scares me."

Helen didn't mind.

The nose of the craft tilted upward and the landing gear tucked into the bowels of the plane. Helen squeezed Blair's hand. "You okay?" Blair nodded.

A sudden and violent yank on Helen's belt told her the worst: wind shear. A wing tipped right. Claws from hell ripped the jet downward. They dropped. One hundred feet. Two hundred feet. Helen knew. No way out. Blair and Helen locked eyes. She pushed Blair down by the shoulder. Sounds of heavy metal clashed with concrete; ten thousand screaming nails on chalkboard scratched a path through darkness.

❖

A burst of wind freckled snow onto Helen's face and awakened her. Dark. Sounds and smells. Sirens wailed; voices screamed. Smoke, fuel. Warmth beneath her. Nerves blasted pain throughout her body, and consciousness fell into darkness.

"Over there!"

She awakened to the shout of a rescue member. A light over her shoulder revealed her provider of warmth.

"Blair," she whispered and closed her eyes.

Jolted conscious again, she heard steel jaws chew through metal behind her.

Alive. An explosion pierced her ears.

"Keep that fire out of here!" a rescue member yelled.

A fine mist dampened her. She felt on fire, and then felt no more until she heard the joyous whoop of her attending emergency medical technician.

"Good heart rhythm," he said. "Gotta watch the BP. Eighty-eight over seventy-three."

A fractured fraction.

Someone switched on the siren and they sped off. Classical music played within the ambulance.

CHAPTER SEVENTEEN

Helen heard distant whispers. Soft footsteps. A squeaky wheel. A closer, intentional voice fully disturbed her sleep. A hand pressed against her shoulder.

"Helen, can you hear me?" a man asked.

Helen tried to speak but wanted more to sleep.

"Do you know where you are?" He grasped her hand. "Squeeze if you can hear me."

She had no energy or desire to squeeze. Helen took a breath. "Hosp'al."

"That's right. I'm Dr. O'Brien, and you've been our surgical guest for the last eight hours. You're in recovery and we'll take you to a room shortly. Do you know what happened?"

"Pla'e. Pla'e," she said again, desperate to complete the word. The longer she remained conscious, the greater her pain from head to toes. Her entire right side felt engulfed in flames. Her flesh boiled. Her head was about to burst from tight bandages. Her teeth hurt. She groaned. "Pai—nuh."

"Pain. Okay. I'll raise your morphine dosage."

She faded out and fell into a slippery slope of muddy dreams. Blair was beneath her. Cory played manically on a piano with no keys. On a wing of the *Princess*, Marty danced a windless ballet. Sam flashed his furry eyebrows. "They could stonewall you."

She had hit the wall.

❖

Was it another day? A different hour? September? Somewhere in time, her oral oxygen tube had been replaced with a simple tube that hissed life-sustaining air into her nose. Voices cluttered her sleep.

"Go ahead, Cory," a woman said, "you won't hurt her."

Her drugged brain processed the name. *Cory. Cory... Chamberlain. Richard Chamberlain. Richard...Cory? He glittered. Bullet in his head.*

Two warm hands cradled Helen's left hand. "I'm here, Helen. Stacey's here. She wants you to come out and play."

An odd beep sounded from an apparatus.

"Her heart is strong," the woman said in reassurance. "Maybe it's her way of saying hello."

"I saw the wreckage in the paper," Stacey said. "I think coverage was greater with Helen and Blair so well known to the public."

Stacey. Friend.

"Names sell," Cory said. "Helen was right about that."

A blanket was placed over Helen's hand. There was a draft on her eyes and lips. The jangling of a cart drew her attention. Beneath closed eyelids, she shifted her eyes toward the sound.

"Your friend is doing well," a different female said. "Helen's breathing is upgraded, but her physician wants to use the external air for a while."

Nurse.

"Has she been awake?" Cory asked.

"Awake, yes. Full of conversation, no. She watched on and off while I sponge bathed her."

"Did she say anything?" Cory asked.

"She was funny. I was changing a dressing on her stomach and she said 'Hurts.' I told her she went through quite an ordeal. Then she said 'Cramps.' I nearly wet my pants from laughing."

Helen's good arm was moved and poked.

"She's blown an IV. I'll get someone from hematology up here."

"Do you suppose she can hear us?" Cory asked.

Helen had been listening, in and out of sleep, but it required too much energy for her to stay awake. Her pain was intense, consciousness bearable only for so long, but she knew Cory was there.

Hello, baby.

She wondered if the crash burned her body. It felt so. Her right side throbbed with pain. Her face was itchy. Curiously, her left side felt good, not restricted by gauze and plaster.

Plaster. What color? And what's that tube? It makes me want to pee. What's the word? I can't think. Catharsis? Cathode? Kathryn Howard? Katherine Parr?

Helen drifted.

"I have work to do," the nurse said. "If you need me, push the button on the wall. I'll turn off the video monitor for now, and you can have some privacy."

Monitor. Catheter. Of Aragon. And Helen slept again.

❖

Quiet room. Hungry. Sunday? Monday?

"I've brought you some scrubs and bath essentials, if you

want to stay the night," a female said. "These aren't chic, but they're fresh. Use Helen's shower if you like."

"Thanks, Linda."

Glitter. She smiled internally.

❖

The scent of generic soap grew stronger and stung Helen's nose. The sound of a chair dragged across the floor, came close, and stopped at her bed. Two warm hands took hold of hers.

"I'll stay with you tonight," Cory said.

Helen summoned enough strength to squeeze Cory's hand.

"Helen? Can you talk to me?"

Helen slowly opened her eyes and looked at her for the first time in—*how long*? It took all of her power, but she managed to pull Cory's hand to her lips. She kissed a finger, not knowing if it was her hand, or Cory's, her lips had touched.

"Sorry," Helen whispered, tears in her eyes.

"For what?"

"Boston," she managed to say.

"It's not your fault."

"Burned?" She struggled to touch her bandaged face.

Cory shook her head. "No. Your nose is broken."

"Blair?" When Cory didn't answer, Helen knew.

"We'll talk about Blair when you're feeling better."

"Luhfyoo." Her bandages caught her tears. She closed her eyes, welcoming sleep.

Cory nodded. "Luhfyoo, too."

CHAPTER EIGHTEEN

B risk daytime voices nudged Helen from a light sleep. Carts, trays, and dishes clanged and chattered in the hall. The smell of bacon wafted directly to her brain. As much as she wanted to have a meal, sleep remained her best pain reliever.

Footsteps came near her bed.

"Good morning, Helen. It's Dr. O'Brien again," he said. "I have some students with me and we'll review your injuries. Is that okay with you?"

Talk? Her? She forced her eyes open. "Okay," she said with less force than their first meeting.

"Good. I hope you rested well last night. We're going to give you an injection of Demerol first. The nurse will change your bandages during the briefing and you might feel some stinging."

Was he kidding? All through the night, Helen had been stabbed with needles, disturbed with an annoying trucks-backing-up sounds when her monitors went haywire, and subjected to nurses' station laughter from the amiable and bored night shift who took it upon themselves to play Twenty Questions at the expense of her R&R. And who in the hell scheduled her good limbs for physical therapy in the middle of the night? Had she slept well? Yes, a long, long time ago.

Helen didn't answer. The effects of a new dose of pain reliever erased her brain enough to enjoy intermittent moments of rest but also enlightenment to the extent of her injuries.

"Her right side took the brunt of the accident. Her femur was broken in three places, and her foot was nearly severed at the ankle. The ankle has since been rebuilt with titanium and there has been no rejection by the surrounding tissue…

"…slash on her abdomen exposed the colon…no organs were damaged, but the right kidney was bruised…internal bleeding was limited to the bowel…right shoulder dislocated… forearm was broken…multiple lacerations and avulsions…"

I survived this?

Bandages were peeled from her face.

"…broken nose was her only direct facial injury…but she suffered a deep gash from her chin along…general bruising and scrapes along her right side."

"Was she burned?" an unfamiliar voice asked. "Did she suffer any spinal injuries?"

"Surprisingly not," Dr. O'Brien said. "…in and out of consciousness for five days…progress is good…vital signs are holding steadily…turning her over to her private physician… I'll check on her, as will the orthopedic surgeon."

She slept for what felt like hours. No voices came and went. She still smelled bacon, and her mouth watered. The steady rhythm of a monitor lulled her back to sleep.

❖

"She's pleased with the vitals," the nurse said.

"Yes, I am. I'm Dr. Santos, and you are…?"

"Cory Chamberlain."

Helen's ears prickled toward the sound of Cory's voice.

"I'd like to speak to Ms. Chamberlain alone." She removed

the oxygen tube from Helen's nose. "Helen's a good friend of mine, and she's told me about you. It's nice meeting you."

"Thank you, Doctor."

"Teresa."

"Call me Cory. What has she told you?"

"You're lovers."

"Thank God." She sounded relieved. "I won't have to be clever with the way I word questions and answers."

"Helen's chart is remarkable," Teresa said. "Heart rate: sixty-eight. Blood pressure: one twenty-two over eighty. Respiration: seventeen. Temperature: ninety-nine point three. Other than a slight elevation in temperature, do you know what this tells me?"

"She's sleeping," Cory said.

"Exactly. She could have a quick recovery, but her brain tells her to reject the pain. It's acceptable for some people, but I don't want her to hide. I've been her physician for twelve years. I know her body and habits. If she's conscious and dealing with her injuries, she'll be out of here in record time."

"Nobody wants to be aware of pain. She knows what she's doing," Cory said. She took Helen's left hand into hers.

"I have no doubt. It wouldn't even surprise me if she was listening."

Damn.

"What do you suggest, then?"

"You could wake her up."

"Can I do that?"

"Why not?"

"She looks so fragile. Can't we let her sleep?"

Sleep. Night-night.

"She's hiding. Wake her up and she'll recover quickly. That would be the strength of Helen's will."

Will Penny. Penny candy. Candy. I read that. Oh, Daddy.

"I don't want her to hurt."

Teresa countered. "I won't say it again, Cory. Being conscious could mean a vast difference in time for her healing process."

Pasteurized process?

"Why saddle me with this decision?"

"Because you love her. Because you want her back. Think selfishly if you have to."

Appeal to the heart. Double major in psych? Major minor? Major pain.

"You do it," Cory said. "I've already caused her enough pain."

I miss you, baby.

"I'm her physician, and she'll fight me. You're her reason. Go ahead, Cory. Wake her up."

She took a deep breath, grasped Helen's shoulder, and shook it slightly. "Helen," she said with a quiver in her voice.

Teresa was stern. "You aren't going to hurt her. Wake her up."

"I can't."

"Do you love her?"

"Yes."

I love you, baby.

"Do you want her out of this bed?"

"Yes."

"Then wake her up."

"Helen." Cory shook her shoulder with more fervor. "Come on."

"Go on. Don't be nice. Tell her you need her. Tell her to stop thinking about herself."

"It's only been five days!"

"Five days that will turn quickly into five weeks. Damn

it, Cory, wake her up! Take her back. Don't let her have her escape."

Baby?

Teresa wouldn't back off. Helen expected her to tell her to tell Cory to stop acting like a child and get on with it. But instead, gentleness returned to her voice.

"It's all right."

Cory grasped Helen's shoulder tightly.

"Listen to me, Helen. Teresa says you're sleeping too much." She shook Helen's shoulder. "Wake up. We have to get you better."

"Come on out, Helen," Teresa said. Helen shifted an arm. "That's it."

Words were Helen's power, and she fought with association.

It...Stephen King...Kingston Trio...Trilogy of Terror... Karen Black...Gail Brown...Another World...Mac Cory... Cory...Cory's talking...Pay attention.

"You have a show to produce. People need you. I need you." Cory rubbed Helen's healthy arm. "Please wake up."

Helen groaned and her eyes fluttered. Cory brushed her fingers across Helen's left palm. The feeling drove Helen crazy in a conscious state and invited reaction now. Helen squeezed her hand shut and she scratched her palm.

"Do it again," Santos coaxed her, and sounded pleased when Helen shook the second tickle away. "Excellent."

Cory reacted more positively. "Come on, that's it. Wake up, baby."

Helen shifted a leg and slowly turned her head toward Cory's voice. She wanted to come out of her sluggishness. She loathed lying there. She wanted bacon. Come on, brain. Do it. Helen opened her eyes enough to see Cory.

"You're baby," Helen whispered.

"Why did she say that, I wonder?" Teresa asked.

"I never call her baby. That's right." She squeezed Helen's hand. "I'm baby."

"Helen? It's Teresa Santos. Can you turn your head to me?"

Helen turned toward the voice and saw the thick, lush hair of her physician silhouetted from the window's light.

"Yes," she said. "Bitch." She smiled weakly, and reached toward her. Teresa grasped her hand, smiled back, and nodded.

"I can be. Welcome back, Helen. How do you feel?"

"Stomach hurts. Leg hurts here." She pointed to her right thigh. "Face is itchy."

"I can remove your facial bandages, but you have to keep the nose piece. We can't have you breaking it all over again." Teresa carefully removed the gauze and placed it on the table beside the bed. "Does that feel better?"

"Better." She touched the dressings on her jaw and neck. "These?"

"They have to stay. You have a nasty injury."

"Cory?" She turned her head slowly to find her.

"Yeah, I'm here."

"Feed..." She took a shallow breath. "...fish."

Cory kissed her cheek. "I promise."

CHAPTER NINETEEN

After a week of consciousness, Helen had grown increasingly restless and fed up with patient life. Needles were removed from her arm, which was then stabbed with a replacement. Blood withdrawal or IV, it didn't matter. Whoever poked her experienced difficulty in finding a good vein, and it hurt like hell.

Lemon ice was on her list of "get that crap away from me." If she saw another paper cup of frozen yellow in her lifetime, it would be too soon. And broth, although she did appreciate the fresh brew and its miniscule flecks of chicken that floated about. It almost tasted like food. It wasn't bacon, but it filled her tummy.

Physicians wanted her to get more rest, but the hospital remained noisiest during the night. There was no serenity for the ill and recovering, and she'd had enough. Although her strength improved daily from her meager meals and catnaps, as did her stubbornness, she wanted to be released.

She glared at Teresa. "I'm gonna pass out."

"Breathe slowly. You're hyperventilating," she said in a no-nonsense voice.

Translation: If she didn't cooperate and cough up on demand, she would require some serious chest stomping from a nasty head nurse. Clear the lungs or drown.

Reluctantly, she took the plastic piece into her mouth.

After three breaths, she coughed and immediately grabbed her hurting stomach. Thick phlegm escaped from her throat. She spat it into a plastic bowl.

"That's disgusting."

"If you don't cough it up, you'll find yourself in deep shit with an oxygen tent."

Helen narrowed her eyes. "Do you talk to all of your patients like that?"

"Like what?"

"'Deep shit.'"

Teresa laughed. "No. You were comfortable calling me a bitch, so I can say 'deep shit' to you, especially if you're headed that way." She put the plastic to Helen's mouth. "Now, breathe."

Helen watched the white cylinder rise and fall through her treatment. The required 1,500 milliliters mark was only half an inch away. Or was it milli*meters*? How do they gauge air sucking? No matter. Helen could suck air with the best of them.

She filled her lungs, and the cylinder rose to the maximum 2500 mark. A thimble-like gauge to the left shook and shot to the top. Gotta get the prize.

❖

Tinkly sounds of the merry-go-round played in the background as the eight-year-old Helen fired water into her target. The ball moved steadily upward. Gotta have that alligator. Above her target, the furry toy waited.

Wide-eyed with anticipation, she stuck her tongue out past her lips and pulled the trigger tighter. She glanced at her competitors' targets. Number four gained on her, but number seven fell back. The others were nowhere near. She pulled harder. Five was gaining. Three was on her tail. Now neck and neck. Four came up fast.

Helen squeezed with both hands. Zrrring! went the bell. Her heart stopped. She watched the water drain and she looked up at the man who wore a red-and-white apron.

"What'll it be, little girl?" he said to her and waved his cane over the shelves of prizes.

The other kids groaned.

Helen squealed and jumped. "Me? The alligator!" She pointed to the fuzzy reptile and claimed her prize.

❖

Helen coughed and spat another wad of goo into the bowl. Some prize.

"Good." Teresa handed her a glass of water. "Do it again tonight. I'll have the nurse watching, so don't think you'll get away without doing it."

"She can be bought."

Teresa placed the stethoscope to Helen's chest. "Take a deep breath and hold. Now out, hard. Sounds good."

Helen recovered from a cough and gazed out the window. A blue sky hung over New York. She wanted to smell winter's clean air and feel it chill her lungs. She'd had plenty of friends trooping in and out, stacks of get-well cards, and fresh flowers. Endless attention from a particular female aide amused her. She wanted for nothing, but she was ready for civilian status. A plane passed in the distance. Blair flashed in her mind and Helen turned away from the window.

"When can I go home?"

"In about a week."

"Unacceptable. It's already been thirteen days and I'm feeling well enough."

"You've been conscious for only eight of those days." Teresa smiled.

"You're enjoying this, aren't you? It's a control thing, isn't it?" Helen's face grew hot and she flung a pillow. "I damn near blow up my lungs for you and—"

"And what's this ruckus I heard from all the way down the hall?"

Helen swung her head toward the figure in the doorway. A wonderful sight. Cory joined them at the ringside.

"She won't let me go home," the eight-year-old in Helen huffed.

"Wow. No 'Hello, baby' or promises of unconditional love?"

"I'm not in the mood for sentimental sweetness."

Cory raised her eyebrows and glanced at Teresa.

Teresa reached for Helen's nose brace. "Let's see what's behind door number two."

"Am I going to look like a fighter?" Helen grumbled.

"No, but a raccoon comes to mind."

"Wonderful. Ow. Jesus!" she yelled when Teresa peeled away the tape.

"Sorry. There. All done." She placed the piece on the table. "What do you think, Cory?"

Cory motioned with her hands. "I think it leans to the left."

"What?" Terrified that her nose had healed crooked, Helen crossed her eyes in effort to see the damage.

Cory laughed. "That was lovely."

"That isn't funny," she grumbled. Teresa handed her a mirror. "I do look like a raccoon."

"You'll lose the discoloration. Other than that, it's straight as can be."

In the mirror, Helen studied the bandages on her neck and jaw. She reached up to her chin. "Can I see what I look like beneath this?"

Teresa removed packaged scissors and tweezers from her pocket. "Yes, and the surgeon has permitted me to remove the sutures. He's done a nice job and the scar should heal smooth, but right now it's not very pretty." She removed the tape and peeled back the white patches.

Helen turned her head to see her injury in the hand mirror. Red and puffy tufts of flesh stretched from her chin, along her jaw, and down to her collarbone. All held together with black stitching. Her personal barbed-wire fence. No, it wasn't pretty. Makeup would cover the injury, but she couldn't wear makeup to bed. What would Cory think of her now?

Teresa proceeded to remove the black knots and Helen grabbed Cory's hand. Cory would be less attracted to her. She'd run off with some other woman. Some other blonde. One without scars. One who would happily feed her fish. One who would cook for her, sniff blindly at her heels, and follow her to Boston. One who would sleep with her. The heifer.

"Hey," Cory said and moved closer.

Helen looked at her. Go with that blonde, then. Enjoy her Pollyanna complexion. Let her clean up your piles of Rice Krispies. "What?" Helen pouted.

"I love you."

Helen smiled, triumphant over the heifer. "I know. Will you please kiss me?" Cory looked toward Teresa. "It's okay. She knows we sleep together."

Teresa removed the final thread and placed the instruments on the bed table. She laughed and pulled the curtain, separating herself from them. "She's a mean badger today. You better kiss her, or I will."

Helen looked sadly at Cory. "I heard the surgeon describe my injuries. How will it be for you to see a map of Florida on my stomach?"

"I thought you wanted a kiss." Cory leaned into Helen's mouth.

Helen smiled as Cory's lips touched hers. Warm and soft. The heifer won't know what she missed. "I miss you, baby."

"Then get dressed," Cory said. "Sam's waiting with his van."

Helen grabbed a small piece of the curtain and yanked it open. "Really?" she asked Teresa.

"There are rules," she said and looked up from Helen's chart. "Stay in the chair until the ortho surgeon removes the cast. Then it's off to physical therapy with you."

"Okay."

"No sex for now. Touch a little, if you want, but no more. The strain will be too much for your abdomen."

Helen looked at Cory and grunted something close to "Okay."

"Stay on a soft diet and graduate to an intake of your regular meals. Your digestive system will tell you what you can handle. Change the dressings on your leg every two days for a week. Then you can take them off completely. I'll send along a care package of bandages and tapes." She sat on the bed and took Helen's hand. "I'm glad you're okay."

Helen gave her a smile. She wished it could be more. The woman most responsible for her life deserved—what? Eternal devotion? A lifetime of house cleaning service? The History Channel? What would it take to repay her?

"I'm alive because of you." Helen hugged her with all the strength of her one healthy arm. "How do I repay that?"

"You just did." She wrote on her prescription pad, tore the

sheet off, and handed it to Helen. "Call this woman. She's a psychiatrist."

"A shrink?" Helen handed back the paper. "I don't need a shrink."

"Helen." Teresa paused and looked into Helen's eyes. "Honey, you'll experience some degree of emotional trauma. Post-traumatic stress is not a happy place for anyone. I'm told you don't sleep well."

"You didn't tell me that," Cory said.

Helen fidgeted. "I don't sleep well in strange beds, and the floor personnel are loud at night."

"Maybe that's all it is. Hopefully." Teresa handed the paper to Cory. "Just in case, Carolyn Ingram is among the best." She squeezed Helen's hand. "Say you'll call her if you need to talk."

"Just in case, then." Helen turned to Cory. "Take me home, woman."

❖

In the back of Sam's van, Helen fooled with the motorized wheelchair that he had provided. Not much space to burn rubber, but she got the gist of the controller. She also found that if she held the brake, pressed the joystick forward, then released the brake, she could almost pop a wheelie. She'd be hot on Chamberlain's heels without tiring. There she went again, chasing a woman.

Horns blared. Tires squealed outside the van. Helen lurched forward, then fell back and against the chair. She closed her eyes, terrified while the fuselage tore open, and tightened her hand on Blair's shoulder.

Something hit her leg. Helen jumped and opened her eyes.

Cory's hand rested on her knee. Her heart beat wildly while sounds of her New York surroundings came back to her.

It's over. There's no plane. No danger.

"Are you all right? Do you want to stop?" Cory asked.

She lied. "I'm okay. Everything feels and sounds new." She wiped sweat from above her lip. "I'm anxious to get home."

"One more block," Sam said.

❖

The ride through the hallway clinched Helen's desire for home. The familiar smells of the Dakota and the scent of Cory's perfume grew stronger as she approached the apartment. At the hospital, her sense of smell had been limited to clean linen and alcohol swabs. Not to mention bacon.

Sam stopped outside Cory's door. "I'll leave you two alone." He bent down and kissed Helen's cheek. "Welcome home. I'll call you in a couple days."

"Thanks for your help," Helen said.

"You're welcome. Call if you need anything." He hugged Cory. "Take care of my girl."

"I will," she said.

Cory opened the door. Helen motored herself in and stopped. Apprehension. Fear. She remembered the same feelings when she submitted her first column to Sam. Was she good enough? Did she belong there?

Helen thought, this is the world of the living, where people laugh and talk and live and walk. A world where planes crash and people die. I didn't die, or am I spirit? Am I ethereal, refusing to leave a worldly realm? Am I now embracing the living, as I once embraced the dead? Where are the dead if I'm among them?

"They're looking at you," Cory said, pointing to the aquarium.

Helen smiled at their aquatic roommates. She wheeled herself toward the aquarium with its blue and green gravel and the mermaid that lounged on top of a bubbling shell. The filter hummed its sleepy song. Yellow and white coral, tucked into one corner, was home to a bashful swordtail. Helen looked closely and saw him there. She touched the glass.

"Come on out, little guy," she said. He flicked his tail, but Helen knew she'd never get him beyond his fortress. She counted six healthy fish. The new mollies she had bought seemed in their element and swam to Helen's fingertips.

"Look, baby," she said, and Cory crouched beside her. "She's pregnant." She pointed to the mollie's swollen belly. "We'll have to separate her from the others. They'll eat the babies." She turned to Cory. "They're all alive," she said. I'm alive.

"They missed you. You're the one who talks to them."

"You should breakfast with them," Helen said playfully.

Helen leaned forward and pulled Cory closer. She kissed her. A first kiss, a new kiss. The kiss she would always have Cory feel. A kiss that promised love and life. A kiss that would swell and explode in Cory's head, suck the breath out of her, and charge her with a powerful current.

Helen pulled her mouth away. "Hello, you lovely woman."

"Hi," Cory said, flushed from Helen's kiss. "You're here. I don't believe it."

Helen tugged at Cory's jacket. "And I don't believe you're in wool. I'm not going far. Get rid of this outfit and come back to me."

Helen wheeled into the kitchen. Her eyes devoured every plate glass cabinet, every white tile. Maybe one day, a day when Cory was out peddling her talent, Helen would chisel out a block and replace it with a lavender one. It would read: Helen Loves Cory. A Rice Krispie sat alone on the alcove table. Good. She wanted it there, and a few more, if they need be. They were just one of life's little piss-me-offs that she could grumble about and then thank God she was alive to see them.

Cory approached from behind. Helen swung her chair around and rested her eyes on her. The real prize for surviving looked more comfortable and even more adorable in azure blue. She was her reason for living and for loving again. Cory had spent countless hours at the hospital, mothering, humoring, and showing a spark of jealousy over the attentive aide. Now, devoted to the care of Helen, she had canceled her tour until March.

She pulled up a chair and tossed Helen a Fanny Brice smile. The same smile that had flickered through Helen's mind as the fuselage exploded in front of her. Helen's eyes brimmed with tears and Cory held her as best she could.

Cory sobbed. "I thought I might lose you."

Cool hair brushed against Helen's cheek. She moved slowly against it. The scent of fresh shampoo blended with Giorgio's Wings. A citrus garden, a tropical drink, Helen buried her toes into the warm sand.

"I couldn't help but live." Helen stole a deep breath. "Still want to be my girl?"

"Still."

How still it must have been after the crash, after the explosions. So many lives lost. Helen cried in Cory's arms. Deep, painful sobs wracked her body. Her head felt on the verge of its own explosion. "Don't let go," she said. "I feel safe in your arms."

"You're safe, but I think you should call Dr. Ingram. I didn't like your look in the van."

Helen pulled away. "You look good in that shade of blue," she said, but Cory wouldn't buy the flattery.

"I'm serious. I think this is important for you."

"I'll call her. I promise."

❖

Helen slept through most of the afternoon. A sound, peaceful sleep, a gift from whatever angel guarded her. Lemon or honeysuckle tickled at her nose. Warm breath against her forehead would alight and then be gone. She drifted back into sleep and awaited the angel's return.

When she awakened, she was thankful that her place was on the right side of the bed. The farther away Cory was from the facial scar, the better. She traced the tender incision with her finger. From the tip of her chin to the back of her jaw—but she stopped there and thanked God she was alive.

"Hey," Cory said, when she entered the bedroom. "How about a cup of tea?"

"Sounds good."

Cory assisted Helen's move from the bed and into the wheelchair. That was a cumbersome act which included Helen sitting up and entering the chair in the opposite way that she'd left it. There was time and she took advantage. Cory was a saint with her patience.

On the breakfast table, beside her cup of tea, was a manila envelope. In large letters, obviously Stacey's handwriting, was Helen's name.

"What's this?" she asked.

"Stacey gave that to me a few days after your accident.

She asked me to take a look and decide if you should see the contents." She looked at the envelope as though she still weighed the decision. "I've decided you would want to see the photos."

Helen took the envelope and opened it. She reached inside and pulled out a stack of newspaper articles and photographs. Stacey had written a brief cover letter, and Helen read it out loud.

"'Hey, Blondie. I hope you won't regard the pictures as a malicious act on my part. I know the reporter in you, and she always wants the full story. Now you have it. I love you, Stacey.'"

Helen studied the newspaper photos of the plane wreckage. Split and mangled, the entire right side of the fuselage, several hundred yards from the plane's eventual stop, was a blackened shell. Helen's and Blair's seats had been on the left side. That side, nearly crushed like a bug from impact, was circled by rescue vehicles and people.

Okay, that's exactly what Helen had expected to see—carnage, in black and white. She didn't remember the moment of impact, only what she saw in her dreams, and could now remove herself from the photos in spite of her injuries. What she felt was sadness for the seventy-three people who had died. After skimming the articles Stacey had included, she set the papers aside.

"All I know is I'm hurting and these pictures tell me why."

"You missed some. There's another envelope inside."

She found the envelope and withdrew several 5x7 glossy and full-color photos. The first was a side shot of a blanketed and bandaged person. On the next was a full facial shot.

She looked at Cory. "This is me?"

"Stacey took the pictures one day when she was alone with you."

Helen looked back at the bandaged face. "Holy shit."

Purples and blues and reds. A red, ripened summer plum. It was the closest she could come to describing the small area of her face that remained visible. Only around the oxygen tube in her mouth, and the swell of her lips and eyes, was there evidence that she was a living human being, and not the carcass of a soul bound for a funeral pyre.

She looked back at the full-length photo. The sheet that covered her was higher, smoother on the right side, a reminder of the plaster molding beneath it that held her leg together.

In another photo, a heart monitor kept steady rhythm while piggybacked intravenous solutions dripped into long tubes connected to the backs of both hands. Another tube fed blood into her system, while a third led to a smaller bag labeled *Morphine.* Bound by plaster, tubes, and wires, hooked up to life-supporting machines that go beep-beep into the night, she appeared more like a science fiction creation than a woman.

She placed the pictures back into the envelope. "Welcome home, Helen," she said to herself. "Makes me wonder how I survived."

Cory nodded. "But you did, and many people are very happy." She took Helen's hand into her own.

"Did you go to the services for Blair?"

"She was buried at Ferncliff Cemetery, in Hartsdale. I attended with Stacey and Marty. Marty took it hard. She didn't want to leave Blair in a can."

Helen internalized her feelings of guilt. Had she been responsible for Blair's death? She could only come up with a positive response. With that in her mind, she kept the moment light and responded.

"Ferncliff is where Judy Garland and Joan Crawford rest. Harold Arlen. To name a few celebrities. Blair would have loved the idea. She always liked a good ending."

"I'm sure she's still around," Cory said. "She's probably lurking about this apartment, trying to think up ways to piss me off."

Helen smiled a little. "I'm out of energy already. Get me back into bed?"

"Sure, and I'll stay right next to you this time."

CHAPTER TWENTY

Although she was tired at the end of an evening, mornings and afternoons were good for Helen. She wouldn't allow Cory to take pity on her and proved quite capable of doing many tasks.

Those things included keeping a spotless aquarium and well-fed fish, motoring dirty dishes to the dishwasher, watering plants, and any other household chores that she reached from a sitting position. Two weeks went by and she convinced Sam that she was taking fewer pain meds and was well enough to do a weekly column.

The show's group had carried on with their plans during her hospitalization. Stacey had acted as producer-at-large. There was little remaining for Helen to organize, and with plenty of time on her hands, she felt a need to become involved again. Everyone would have a swell time and she'd simply be a hostess. A Suzy Homemaker of the vaudeville kind. No, she couldn't let her role be that miniscule. If she was about to fling herself from the closet, she'd make sure she was their equal, if only for that night. But how? What could she do?

She looked toward the music room and then tapped the cast on her arm. For bathing purposes, the cast was removable. She'd found her answer.

Cory, it turned out, was a creature of habit. She was wired, restless, and baby-sitting was not her forte. Helen sensed her need to perform and that need played along perfectly with her intentions, which included a surprise for Cory.

Cory finished shaving Helen's single hairy leg, rinsed it with warm water, and smoothed cream over the fresh flesh. She topped it off with a kiss to Helen's big toe.

"Thanks, baby," Helen said.

"I enjoyed that. I'll do both someday." She tapped on the cast.

Helen shuddered. "It's frightening to think what we'll find under that one."

Helen took the shaving paraphernalia back to the bathroom and then parked her ride beside Cory. "Do you think we need time away from each other?"

Cory looked away from a book and to Helen. She closed the paperback. "Are you getting tired of me?"

"No. I just think there's no reason for you to coop yourself up every minute for me. I can get around pretty well."

"I would like to get some running in, maybe visit my manager." After a quick thought, she showed more excitement. "Vladimir Ashkenazy is in town this week. I'd love to see him perform and say hello. Are you sure you're okay if I leave you alone for a while?"

"Yeah. Maybe Stacey or Marty will drop in. Maybe Yoko." She smiled. "No, really. Enjoy yourself."

Cory agreed.

❖

Although Helen felt guilty for her harmless scheme, several hours each week were filled with nine feet of grand piano, and Marty who usually arrived right after Cory left. When Cory returned from an outing, she talked amicably with

Marty, but there was a small cloud of coolness that alerted Helen to a problem.

"I'm tired," Cory once said when Helen asked if something was wrong. "We don't have much in common," was her most interesting response.

"You're both artists, entertainers, known to practically all nine planets, and you think you have nothing in common?"

Helen shrugged off Cory's attitude and attributed it to winter doldrums.

Three weeks later, Marty finished reading aloud the latest chapter of a lesbian novel, while Helen practiced the left hand to Beethoven's "Moonlight Sonata." She'd chosen the piece for the memory of Cory in the Jacuzzi, and also because of its simplicity on the lower register of the piano.

"Why do I have to read this mushy stuff to you?" She flung the book toward Helen. "It's about a green woman."

"She's a witch who's in love with a mortal, and Cory thinks I'm reading when she's out. You read, I listen, and I learn the sonata at the same time. I tell Cory about the book, and everybody is happy."

Marty collapsed to the floor and stretched her leg muscles. "Not me. That romantic stuff makes me ill. Give me horror. Bite my neck and send me screaming into the night." She expressed amusement when Helen stopped her practice and grinned. "I haven't seen a smile like that since Carter was president."

"There was a time when I would have bitten your neck."

"Well, sweetheart." Marty stopped exercising and shuffled up to her. "Let's get you into bed." She fooled with the brake on the wheelchair, a playful attempt to grant the wish of yesteryear.

She slapped at Marty's hand and laughed, then held her aching belly. "Was. I said was."

"All right, but if you and Chambermaid ever split—"

"I'll be sure to let you know." Helen returned to the music, while Marty continued stretching. "Listen," she said. With both hands, she played. To her ear, it was slow but promising. She played to the thirty-eighth measure and stopped. "What do you think?"

"It sounds nice." Marty grabbed the coat she'd flung over a chair. "I have to go." She kissed Helen's cheek and headed to the front door. "You're looking much better every time I see you, and life with Cory seems to agree with you. Bye-bye."

Helen nodded and practiced an appropriate fingering for what could be a sloppy run up a series of keys. On her third attempt, she stopped and wheeled back into the living room.

"Hey," Cory said when she entered the apartment and closed the door quietly. She pushed off her running shoes.

"Hi, you. You're covered in snow."

"It's crazy out there. Traffic's at a crawl and my exercise turned into a power walk."

Her wintery cheeks tugged at Helen's need to feel fresh air swirl in her lungs. She was still bound to the chair, so asking for an hour in the snow was out of the question. Helen glanced out the window. She'd wait for better weather.

Cory reached for her jacket zipper. "The storm should end around—"

"Will you take me to the park?" Helen blurted and wheeled to her side. "Let's build a snowman. We'll catch snowflakes on our tongues." She might have sounded like she'd taken too many meds. The idea was crazy and Cory hadn't responded with the least bit of interest. "Never mind. I'll wait."

"I'll take you. The park roads are reasonably clear," Cory said without much enthusiasm, and rummaged through the closet. "I can at least get you over to Strawberry Fields. Give me a minute to find some warm woolies for you."

There was something on Cory's mind, of that Helen was certain, but she didn't let it burst her bubble of freedom that she was about to experience.

"Thanks, baby. This means a lot to me."

❖

Bundled and cozy in a coat, hat, blankets, and mittens, and well beyond Ono's mosaic "Imagine" tribute to John Lennon, Helen sat within Central Park. The setting was a winter wonderland. Heavy snow settled quickly and turned her lap and leg into porcelain art. She didn't care that January's winds stung her cheeks and frosted her breath, but intermittent seconds of the snowy night of the plane crash smashed at her brain. The cries of a baby, the groans of adults. Blair.

"Are you all right?" Cory asked.

"Yes. Just…thinking about that night." And the fire. Smoke that choked her. She held back her tears. "I often wonder why I'm alive."

Cory crouched beside her. "Because you're strong and because you were very fortunate." She slipped her hand beneath the blanket and held Helen's hand. "Have you talked with the psychiatrist?"

"Not yet. I'll call her soon."

"Would you rather leave? Go back to the Dakota?"

"No." She smiled. "Let's finish the snowman."

Cory rolled another ball of snow. Helen took deep breaths and geared her mind back to the beauty, the fun, and of the lives and land that surrounded her.

She poked stones into the snowman to form his jacket.

Then she changed her mind. "I want a snow woman," she said in a matter-of-fact tone, and scooped up enough snow from her lap to form the beginning of breasts.

Cory stepped back and studied Helen's handiwork. "Definitely double Ds." She looked down at her chest and then back to Helen. "You like big boobs."

"Love 'em." Helen growled, then reached for Cory's breasts.

Cory jumped away and looked around quickly. "There are people here."

"So what? New York is full of weirdos." Helen reached again and Cory pushed her hand away.

"Stop it," Cory snapped. "I'm not a weirdo." She moved to the back of the transgender statue.

"Nice knockers," a guy yelled as he jogged by.

"See? Weirdos." Helen continued to form the double D breasts. "Lighten up."

"I suppose Marty would…" Cory's voice trailed off.

Helen stopped and looked around the snowman, at Cory. "She would what?"

"Nothing."

"No, not nothing." Helen wheeled herself to the other side. "What about Marty?"

"All gooey-eyed," Cory muttered.

"Gooey-eyed?"

"Why does she call you so late?" Cory asked.

"She's worried about me."

"I'm there. Tell her not to."

"Tell her not to call?"

"Tell her not to do anything. When I go out, she's usually there when I return, or she's just left. I've seen her leave on several days and evenings. Today I saw her."

"Don't be silly," Helen said lightly. "I understand where it could look bad, though."

"Damn it, Helen. She's always there." She stabbed a branch into Ms. Frosty's side to form an arm.

Helen glared. "Is that an accusation?"

Cory looked at her. "Is there guilt?"

"What?" Helen flung a handful of snow at her. "Sure." She steamed. "I climb right out of this chair and slip into our bed with her. I don't think so." She pushed the top of the snowman with her good arm. Ms. Frosty crumbled on top of Cory's feet.

"Don't talk to me in that tone."

"Do you realize what you're asking me?" She brushed the new layer of snow off her lap. "I happen to love you."

"Marty's your fantasy. Maybe you're connecting the dots?"

Helen stared. "I don't believe you said—"

"I won't be used, Helen."

"Used? You think I'm using you? I'm not listening to this." She maneuvered a crisp left turn with her chair and headed toward Central Park West.

"Come back here!" Cory yelled.

"Get real," Helen called over her shoulder.

"You don't have your key."

"And you don't have a clue."

Helen chastised herself while her wheels skipped and slid beneath her. *Why did I ever say Marty was my fantasy? Of course she'd think we're fooling around. It's her fear of being used. This is my fault.* She quickly flip-flopped. *Bullshit. She should trust me.*

Cory caught up to Helen and they plodded through the fresh powder.

"Why don't you trust me?" Helen bellowed.

"I don't trust her. She can be charming."

"And I'm a sucker for charm?"

"Are you?"

Helen let go of the joystick, skidded to a stop, and looked over her shoulder.

"Shove it." She spun off again.

Back and forth, their battle continued through the park. Helen denied this and Cory suggested that until, what seemed an eternity getting through the park, they reached the outside perimeter of the trees. Cory stopped.

"Now look what we've done," Cory said, sounding helpless.

"Fought," Helen mumbled, looked to her left, and then she stopped as well. The Metropolitan Museum of Art laughed at both of them. "Damn it. We're on Fifth Avenue."

Cory turned the chair around for Helen and they silently headed back across the park.

"Are you warm enough?" Cory asked, halfway home.

"Very."

Without another word uttered between them, they reached the elevator at the Dakota. Helen was angry, tired, cold, and hungry. The doors closed and she pushed a button.

"That's the wrong floor," Cory grumbled, and hit the button for the fourth floor.

"Maybe I'm going to Yoko's."

"Whatever. I'll leave the door open."

She was quiet again until the elevator chimed, then she held the door and waited before following. Cory tucked herself into her music room, while Helen made tea and fixed a light supper.

"Charming." Helen mimicked Cory's description of Marty.

She sliced a grapefruit in half, sprinkled salt over the sections, added cherry halves, and slammed them into the broiler. The cherries skidded to the bottom of the stove.

"I'll give her gooey-eyed." She tore open a bag of fresh biscuits and searched the refrigerator for honey. "Look, you!" She held the jar accusingly toward the music room. "It's crystallized. How many times have I told you not to put the honey in the fridge?" She ran the jar lid under hot water before she could remove it. Holding the jar between her knees, she opened it with her one good hand. Finally, she shoved the glass container into the microwave, and watched it go around and around.

Leaving her own dinner on the alcove table, she wheeled Cory's into the music room and placed the tray on top of the piano.

"Eat," she said.

"Don't leave." Cory reached for Helen's hand.

"Leave me alone," she said and wheeled out.

❖

After picking at her grapefruit, and then taking a warm sponge bath, Helen struggled with putting on a fresh nightgown and pulled herself into bed. She heard the television tuned to the eleven o'clock news.

She opened a Katherine Forrest mystery, read two pages, and then closed the book. Mystery wasn't her favorite genre. She didn't even know where the book came from. Stacey probably left it. She looked at the cover.

"Sorry, Katherine. I don't care whodunit." She tossed the book onto the nightstand and thought about their argument.

Marty ignited a genuine fear in Cory. She felt threatened, but had no idea what Marty's presence actually meant. She'd seen them talking, laughing, kissing good-bye. Of course, the kisses landed on cheeks, but it still looked bad.

Minutes later, Cory came into their bedroom. She removed a nightgown from the armoire and began to undress. She kept her back toward Helen.

"Don't do that," Helen said softly. She scanned the feminine curves in front of her.

"Don't do what?" Cory asked curtly.

"Don't turn from me. Let me see your body."

Cory stood bare from the waist up. She rested her forearms against the armoire and crossed her wrists. She leaned her forehead against them. Her shoulders raised and lowered with each breath she took. When she turned, Helen reached for her.

"Come here, baby." To Helen's disappointment, she stayed across the room.

"We can't fix anger with sex, and Dr. Santos said no."

"Baby, please finish undressing for me."

Helen watched while she stripped. She stepped out of her jeans and panties, and then turned to face Helen. Helen watched and absorbed every inch of her: breasts to sigh for when pondered, to beg for when close to Helen's lips; rounded hips that led to a sweet treasure, hidden behind a curly trim of dark hair.

Cory took a step closer. Helen swallowed when a twinge hit her thighs and she shifted her legs. More than a month had gone by since they'd last made love. The twinge turned to throbs. Helen breathed through her lips and wet them with her tongue.

"How does it feel to want me and not have me?"

"Painful," Helen said, barely audible. "Pleasantly painful, looking at you now."

Cory slipped her toe under her bikini pants. With a quick

kick, they sailed through the air and came to rest across Helen's chest. Helen grabbed the pink microfiber and held it against her lips. She closed her eyes.

When she opened her eyes, Cory stood beside the bed. She took Helen's left hand and Cory pressed it between her legs. When Helen reached for another touch, Cory dropped her hand.

"You want something from me?" she asked, and backed away. She tore the elastic from her hair and shook it loose.

"You are so fine. Yes, I want something."

Cory stepped to the bed again and Helen reached once more. Cory took back Helen's hand.

"A warm, wet place. That's what you want?" She took Helen's index and middle fingers into her mouth, all the way.

"Oh God." Helen groaned as Cory's tongue and lips teased her fingers. Helen pulled back with her hand and slid her fingers in again. Cory parted the fingers with her tongue. She sucked and licked between them, confusing Helen on who seduced whom. "Yes. That's what I want."

She removed Helen's hand and placed the wet fingers inside of her. She put one knee on the bed and allowed Helen to push deeper.

"Oh, baby. You're so wet."

"Do you want to taste me?"

"Desperately."

Cory pulled away from Helen's fingers. She took Helen's hand and brushed the wet fingers against her lips. Helen eagerly took them into her mouth.

"Mmm," she moaned, and her thighs ached to feel Cory's tongue within them.

Cory leaned down. "This isn't fair to you." She breathed hot air against Helen's ear. She sucked gently on an earlobe and traced the edge with her tongue.

Helen groaned loudly and removed Cory's fingers from her mouth.

"I don't care," she said and pulled Cory's mouth onto hers.

They kissed feverishly, and they battled with their tongues until Helen pushed the pillows from the bed. She scooted downward, closer to the end of the bed.

"Get up here." She pulled on Cory's arm, and Cory attempted to stretch beside Helen. "No." Helen patted her chest. "Up here. Straddle me. Do it now."

Cory moved deftly, avoiding Helen's injured arm. She grasped the headboard and lowered herself. Helen grabbed Cory's hip with her good hand and quickly pulled her against her mouth.

"Oh God, Helen." She breathed heavily as Helen swiftly moved her tongue.

Helen bit into Cory's lips. "It's as though I've never tasted you before this." She pressed her cheek against the wetness. She licked wide, slowly. Cory grabbed onto Helen's head and moved swiftly against her mouth. Helen flicked her tongue against Cory's clit and Cory suddenly came. Helen slipped a finger inside to feel the muscle contractions. With each contraction and release, she pulled Helen deeper.

"Oh, yes. Oh, Helen." She gritted her teeth and each groan grew louder until a final shudder told Helen to stop.

Helen reached up with one hand and placed it against Cory's chest. She felt her heart pounding against her fingers. Cory's eyes remained closed while her breaths became normal. She touched Cory's breast and then she grasped it roughly.

"I love your breasts." She squeezed again.

Cory whimpered and then looked downward. The intensity in her eyes hadn't subsided, nor had her quick breaths, but she smiled at Helen.

"My God. That was indescribable."

"Happy to be of service," Helen said lovingly. "Come down beside me."

Cory released the headboard and snuggled closely to Helen's left side. She placed her hand beneath Helen's nightshirt and then between Helen's legs. She massaged gently.

"Just let me touch you," she said. Helen nodded and held on to Cory's arm. "I miss your body." She withdrew her hand and traced circles around Helen's breasts. She grasped Helen's left breast and nuzzled against it. "I didn't hurt you, did I?"

"No," she said. "I'm okay."

"I'm sorry for the fight." Cory nuzzled closer.

"I love you, Cory." Helen struggled to her side and faced her.

"I know. I just—"

"Baby, Marty and I are friends. Tomorrow I'll show you why she's been here so often."

"You don't have to prove—"

She placed her fingers to Cory's lips. "Yes," she said, "I think I do, and I want to show you."

❖

The next afternoon, Helen explained her reading time and treated Cory to a select part of the Townsend talent. The best part, Beethoven, she still kept secret.

After a quick struggle with her removable cast, under the glare of Cory's disapproving eyes, Helen wheeled her chair to the piano and was off with a memorized Bach minuet. She followed with a Burgmüller piece, for which Cory turned the pages.

"That was great." Cory pulled the piano bench alongside Helen. "Do the Bach piece again."

Helen played, and on the third measure, Cory joined in with what Helen could only describe as a dark-side version, and the contrast worked.

"It was tough to learn this," Helen said. "You're so damned good. This stuff flies from your hands."

"It helps that I've been playing since I was four. We all have unique talents. You could write five hundred humorous words on the practical use of tampons versus napkins and I can't write myself out of a bubble."

"Maybe you're right." Helen slowly picked out a tune on the keys. "Do you know this?"

"Very well. It's a Chopin etude. Opus ten, number three. I've never played that piece in public, or for anyone, for that matter."

"Why not? It's so lovely."

"I think it was meant for someone special. Not an audience."

Helen wasn't special? But she didn't pursue it.

"Baby?" She gave Cory a stern look. "Don't accuse me again. I love you. Nobody, nothing, will change that."

Helen had not only quieted Cory's fears about Marty, she had also convinced her that what she had just played was the extent of her talent, enough to get by for the show. The sonata was a secret and, of that secret, there was still much to learn.

CHAPTER TWENTY-ONE

Helen kept her promise and called Carolyn Ingram. They'd agreed to phone sessions, during which Helen talked about her guilt and dreams. Nightmares pummeled her brain. They scratched and bit into her sleep.

For weeks, almost nightly, Helen tossed and rolled, banged Cory with her casts, became soaked with perspiration. A pull on the blankets was a tug on Helen's seat belt. The wind outside the Dakota was the wind that whipped across Helen's bleeding face.

Early in their sessions, Carolyn explained that the dreams might be with her for the rest of her life, but that they would become less frequent and gentler as time passed.

Carolyn also told her a time would come when she could laugh, knowing she had defied death at tremendous odds. It wouldn't mean Helen didn't care about the lives that were lost, only that she had overcome the guilt of survival.

❖

"Blair!" she yelled through the noise of tearing metal and screams.

She reached with her arm, struggled to push Blair

downward. She was blinded by a fiery flash and thrown to the left when the front of the fuselage tore away.

Helen's heart beat boldly while she caught her breath. The dreams were too vivid. She experienced her pain over and over and she wondered if she was meant to come out of sleep. Her dreams became late punishment for her survival. Due justice for the infant who perished.

Cory returned from the bathroom. She turned on the table lamp near Helen and handed her a glass of water and a small hand towel.

"Sometimes I dream only about the water that poured over me. I shivered from the cold. Blair was…dead…or dying… and I stole as much of her body heat as I could. Maybe she'd be alive if I hadn't been selfish." She wiped her sweaty and tear-streaked cheeks.

"Blair's injuries were far less than yours. The coroner said she died of cardiac arrest. You helped her and she might have survived, but you couldn't shield her from fear."

"If I hadn't felt her warmth, I think I might have given up." She sipped from her glass. "I remember hearing Chopin in the ambulance."

"'No pollen haze.' That's what you said to the attendant."

Helen chuckled at the thought. "Really? That's almost embarrassing. With my guts hanging out, I hated it even then." It felt good to find some humor.

"And such a wonderful piece. I think you were jealous that night I kept playing it."

"Jealous over music? Come on. Well, a little, maybe." Helen gave her a playful pout. "But I had you for the rest of the day." She set the water on the table. "Baby, we have five weeks before the show. I know you're restless, and you've been better at going out, but why not see if your manager can reschedule some of your show dates?"

"I canceled to be here for you."

"And I adore you for it, but we need play time together. You know…a cruise, a trip to Kalamazoo…something other than this building. I can't do that right now. Call Liz."

"There isn't enough room in the aquarium for the new fish you'll saddle me with."

"I'll buy you a larger one," she said with a grin.

"I don't want to leave you alone. You still need the wheelchair."

Helen ran her fingers over Cory's cheek. "And you still need the stage. Stacey will baby-sit if I need her. Maybe Yoko."

Cory raised an eyebrow. "And Marty, I assume."

"And Marty. She's a good friend."

The phone rang, and Helen looked at Cory. Yoko? The time was past midnight, an odd hour for conversation. Probably a wrong number.

"Let the machine get it," Helen said.

Two more rings and they recognized Stacey's insistent voice.

"Pick up. It's important."

"What's wrong?" Helen asked when Cory hit the intercom.

"I've been listening to the conversations around the bar tonight. Someone talked to the press about the show."

Helen watched Cory become very busy with straightening a bathroom that didn't need straightening.

"One of us?" Helen asked.

"Maybe Colgate's live-in. They broke up a couple days ago. I can't get Jenny on the phone."

"Do you know who they talked to?"

"No, but sniff around to your colleagues. Maybe get a lid put on it. Whoever it was, they named names."

"Thanks. I'll get on the phone tomorrow."

Cory stood in the doorway. Helen recognized it as the same look she'd had when she was concerned about Marty.

"Come here," Helen said and pulled back the blankets for her. Cory climbed under. "Tell me what's going on behind your pretty green eyes."

"I'm not ready for this."

"Are you having second thoughts about the show?"

"I've realized that I don't want to wake up tomorrow and find myself named as someone's hot tip on page four."

Helen reached for her. "I can't do anything about it until the morning. Try to put it out of your mind."

"How? My reputation is at stake."

"It'll mean your reputation on show night as well."

Cory looked at Helen. "It happened when I was a senior in high school."

"What happened?"

"I opened my locker and there was a note hanging there. It said 'Cory and Lisa are queer.' I wanted to climb inside the locker and never come out. That's the feeling I have now."

"I know that feeling. We all do. That's why we need to come out. To make it easier for the next person. We can be each other's strength, baby."

"How can you be so calm?"

"For the most part, I've stopped being afraid of who I am."

"I'm not backing out, Helen."

"Good. Try to sleep, then. I'll make some calls the first thing in the morning."

Cory turned off the light. Helen held her closely, keeping

her safe from whatever demons lurked in her mind. They didn't talk, but Cory was awake, tossing and turning, and probably seeing that locker open again and again.

When Helen finally slept, she dreamed of pushing on Blair, but it was Cory in the seat next to her. Cory opened her belt and stood up. The plane dropped.

"This isn't safe," Cory said.

Helen watched Cory walk down the aisle and into the fireball.

CHAPTER TWENTY-TWO

Helen hung up the phone, satisfied with the information Sam furnished. The leak was given to Amanda Read, and that told Helen two things: A, the big mouth knew little about Amanda's reporting style, and B, Cory would feel less threatened than if the leak had been told to anyone else.

The fact that it was Amanda was good fortune in its finest moment. It wasn't without reason that she was the biggest in the industry for her gossip column. Amanda wasn't a career breaker. She would scrap an item if she felt it more slanderous than entertaining.

Helen motored herself to the kitchen alcove. Fresh coffee, toast, and fresh sliced pineapple waited on a table set for a queen. A crystal and silver morning was a wondrous change from the preceding night. Cory sat there, proud of herself. Helen pulled up beside her chair and gave her a kiss.

"You're sweet," Helen said and kissed her again. "I love you."

"This is my thank-you-for-loving-me breakfast table."

"And a fine table it is."

Helen looked into Cory's eyes. Sparkle had replaced fear. Once more in her white sweats and with her hair tied back in a Peggy Sue ponytail, Cory was deliciously edible. Right after coffee, Helen would gobble her up. She'd crawl out of her casts and metal brace and that horrible scar on her chin and throat. She would take Cory into her arms and have her, bite after tender bite, leaving nothing but a lovely memory of the woman who had stolen her heart.

"What did Sam say?" Cory asked.

"He said it was Amanda Reed. I called and gave her our address. She'd already told Sam that she thought she should talk to me."

Cory flashed her trademark Fanny Brice smile. "Our address?" She grabbed cream and sugar from the counter.

Helen rolled her eyes and laughed. "Yes, our address. She'll be here at two."

Cory danced over to Helen. "Our address, as in yours and mine?" she asked eagerly. "So you've moved in?"

"You're a pest." Helen tweaked Cory's nose.

"But you love me and it's our address. You said so."

Helen brushed Cory's bangs away. "Do you want me forever, my sweet woman?"

"Forever, Helen."

"When Amanda leaves, we'll discuss the possibilities."

Helen figured Amanda, with her short, salt-and-pepper hair, was in her early fifties. She looked motherly, in an elegant way. They'd met at a charity auction sponsored by the local papers, but that was the extent of their relationship.

"You're looking well, Helen," Amanda said. "The city was worried about you."

"I'm getting along. I'll be out of the chair soon."

"I guess you know why I'm here." Amanda looked at Helen and then at Cory. "I got a call from some young twerp. Frankly, she mentioned a 'coming out' show and told me you two are lovers. She wanted me to fix it so Cory wouldn't be accepted to the Boston Light Orchestra. Can you imagine that?" Amanda laughed.

Helen locked eyes with Cory. She could almost hear Cory's heart pound from ten feet away.

"Excuse me. I'll get the coffee." Cory abruptly stood and they watched her leave the room. Amanda looked back at Helen.

"I struck a nerve. The story's true, isn't it?" Amanda whistled. "I just thought this was a great opportunity to meet you out of the professional air. I never—"

"Don't use the story. We'd like to remain anonymous until the show," Helen said.

Amanda studied Helen curiously, shook her head. "I want to say you don't look like a lesbian, but that's too much of a cliché, even for me."

Helen took a breath. "You can make or break us."

"I could, couldn't I?" Amanda shook her head. "Come on, Helen, you know my reputation. I'm not a bitch."

"Cory's probably thinking the opposite right now."

She looked toward the kitchen. "I feel terrible. Get her in here."

The door swung open and Cory placed the tray on the coffee table. Her color was back.

"Cory, you don't have to worry about me. I won't use the piece."

"I know. I listened at the door. Thanks, Amanda." She poured the coffee and sat with them.

Amanda drank from her cup. "It all makes sense now. The commotion over your columns—especially the black sheep column. I couldn't figure out what you were doing."

Helen shrugged. "Rabble-rousing. Who was your source?"

"Mustn't tell; you know that." She picked up a scone.

Helen let the question remain unanswered and trusted Amanda with her information. After a half hour of friendly conversation and two servings of coffee, Amanda looked at her watch.

"I have to run. Mondays are my busiest days and I still have a Joey Buttafuoco piece to finish."

"People still read that stuff?" Cory asked.

"They eat it up." Amanda rose and walked over to Helen. "I'm happy to see you're doing well." She turned to Cory. "And don't worry about me. I hope you'll knock New York's socks off."

❖

The moment Amanda had mentioned Boston, Cory became another woman. Helen felt the tension throughout the week, and Cory never mentioned the possibility of Helen moving in permanently. Her fear stayed, even with Amanda's reassurance, just as the high school locker had stayed open for all of those years. Cory suddenly didn't like the idea of exposure. Any time Helen made a comment concerning the show and its closeness, Cory would either shrug or make no acknowledgment.

Not until Thursday afternoon did Cory perk up. Helen was in the bedroom and heard her whistling and bustling about. Helen joined her in time to see her pop a champagne cork.

"What's the celebration?" She held the glasses while Cory poured.

Fanny Brice was back, alive and well. "I've been invited to a tea party."

"You've heard from Boston?"

"You're looking at the new maestro for the Boston Light Orchestra." They clinked their glasses and sipped.

Helen was thrilled for Cory. A dream come true, now clenched tightly in Cory's hand. Boston waited for their new conductor and April first was her expected date of arrival.

March sixth was the group's show date, and that left plenty of time in between for Boston to forfeit its decision, should attitudes be swayed. Helen wondered if that would be legal.

"It's nearly show time, baby." She picked up the letter, scanned the page, and looked at Cory. "This is something you've wanted longer than you've known me."

Cory sat on the sofa. "I love you."

"I have no doubt about that." She placed the letter on the table and leaned back into her chair. "But I think you have a serious decision to make. I don't want a life with you where I have to tuck you away into a closet. What do you want?"

"I want you and Boston."

"With me, you could lose Boston."

Helen followed when Cory walked into the music room and sat on the piano bench. She easily pushed back the keys cover and played a delicate minuet.

"I hide in my sleep and you hide in your music. What are you feeling?"

"I'm afraid of losing the position if I do the show. I don't want to get another letter saying they'd made a mistake." Cory stopped the musical piece and rested her hands on her lap. Helen watched tears fall from her eyes. "Telling you isn't easy."

"I need you on stage with me," Helen said quietly.

"If we can't be together, I'll have to live with that. I love you, but—"

"Cory, there's no 'but' in 'I love you.'"

"I care too much what people—"

"Baby, we belong together."

"I can't do your show, Helen."

Helen's heart sank after hearing no protestations or no "screw the world, we should be together." No emotion. Helen grabbed Cory's hand.

"You can't mean this."

Cory sat quietly and touched the piano keys. Helen grabbed the cover, slammed it down, and Cory jerked her hands away in time. The echo was loud in the room, as loud as the look of fear that drenched Cory's face.

"Damn you, Cory Chamberlain," Helen shouted. "Damn you and fuck your piano." She pounded her fist on top of the grand instrument and the strings vibrated their angry response. "I trusted you would be with me that night."

"I'm sorry. It doesn't mean I love you any less."

"You're sorry? You were wrong when you said you couldn't write yourself out of a bubble. You've managed to write yourself out of this one quite nicely." She pounded the piano again.

"We're giving each other room."

"I don't want room from you, baby."

"Then don't do the show."

"I have to. I'm tired of the lies."

"Can't we compromise? Why do they have to know about me?"

Helen laughed. "Let's just rewrite lesbian history. We'll start with Stein and forget to mention Toklas."

"Don't be ridiculous, Helen."

"And you're being a shit. Fine. Have your damn music." Helen spun her chair around and started for the doors, but stopped halfway. She cried. "How can you do this?"

"Don't leave." Cory came up behind her. "You said the

position in Boston is my dream. That's true, but you're the woman for me and I don't want us to part over this. We need to talk and come up with a solution."

"I've compromised my entire life." Helen turned her chair to face Cory. "And now I can't trust you."

❖

With Stacey's assistance, Helen returned to her own apartment. She'd felt her life had seeped out of her, that she'd left it at the Dakota. Cory had become her life and there was nothing wrong with that as long as they hadn't lost themselves in the other. Neither of them did, and that's what separated them.

"Call me when you get home," Helen's answering machine played back. Cory's voice was tired.

Helen didn't call. She wanted to be alone, to whine, to cry, to make some sense out of her last few hours and decide what she should do to make things right. An hour later, the phone rang.

"Hello," Helen said.

"This isn't supposed to happen, Helen. You're overreacting."

"Then be with me. Keep your promise."

"I can't take the risk."

"But you're willing to risk me?"

"I'm willing to compromise. You come out, I stay in."

"We've had this discussion. I won't hide you. I refuse to live that way. What aren't you hearing?"

"That you love me enough to comp—"

"You need a larger vocabulary." Helen was quiet. "You lied to me."

"I didn't lie. I'm scared."

"Then stay in your closet. Go out and play when you can. The world will be proud of you. Good-bye."

Helen hung up, once more betrayed by love. Chasing turned to caring turned to loving turned to leaving.

"Why did I even bother?"

She wheeled herself to the window, opened it, and took a deep breath. She looked to the snow-covered concrete below. She'd survived a plane crash. Would it hurt to jump? What was a little more pain? Who would be there to care? Stacey would. Marty would. Sam. Cory would be happily off to Boston, chased by a heifer. No. She wouldn't give either one the satisfaction.

"'Keep passing the open windows,'" she quoted, and closed the window. "Thank you, John Irving."

She motored to the telephone, punched in Carolyn Ingram's number, and waited.

"Carolyn, it's Helen Townsend. I know it's late—"

"It's okay. Talk to me."

She laughed lightly. "I've been flirting with an open window."

"What's happened?"

"Cory. We fought...I said fuck your piano...we broke up," Helen yelled. "Damn her! She promised me!"

"Promised what?"

"To appear in the show."

"She's changed her mind? Is that what you mean?"

"Yes. She's afraid she'll look bad."

"It sounds to me like she's protecting her future. You can't force her, Helen. That's emotional blackmail."

Helen had no response.

"How are you feeling?" Carolyn asked.

"What the hell kind of question is that? I'm angry and hurt. I'm pissed off. Those are my emotions. Cory's my life and she didn't seem to care about how she's suddenly changed our lives. I can't compromise."

"But she did care. She wanted to talk and you blew her off. Maybe you should think about your reaction to her."

Carolyn listened for several minutes while Helen spit and sputtered, cried, and stomped her one good leg.

"I just wanted to jump. There's always too much pain and upset in love and life."

"Windows are for clarity, not for jumping. You're a survivor in many ways. I want you to rest tonight. Take a Seconal if you have to."

"Sure. Zombie myself out. The World According to Helen."

"Helen," Carolyn said firmly, "take something to help you relax. Even if it's a shot of bourbon."

Helen laughed. "I wanted to jump from a window and you want me to reach for pills and liquor?"

"I can tell by your tone that you aren't going to hurt yourself. Your emotions needed an outlet and you called. That was the right thing to do. I can trust you with some form of a downer. Tomorrow, I want you to call Cory. Sort things out with her. Then, if you still need to talk, call me. I don't care about the time. Just call me."

"Thanks. I will."

Helen hung up and let out a long sigh. She looked around her apartment. It looked exactly as it did before she met Cory. Tan carpet, cream walls, brown furniture, and a piano in the corner. No life. Not even a plant. It needed more color, perhaps. Lavender. Lavender with little pink triangles dotting the walls.

"I think not," she said, then she went into the bedroom and flipped on the light. Right away, she saw what she'd left behind. Life. Over her bed hung an enlarged photograph Stacey had taken one day when Helen and Cory had felt adventurous. An identical copy hung in Cory's bedroom. It was a nude shot, from the waist up.

The black-and-white photo displayed Cory lying in bed with an oversized pillow beneath her head. With her hair splashed around, the look of a woman who had just made love was projected. Helen leaned over Cory, resting on one arm, and their breasts touched lightly. Their mouths were open, nearing a kiss.

Helen remembered the day that seemed moments ago. She still felt Cory's fingers slide against her cheek and pull her downward.

Theirs was a perfect photograph. Loving, sensual, provocative. It made you want to hold somebody. The photograph of the actual kiss was not as powerful, but the kiss itself Helen remembered well. Cory always kissed her as if for the first time. The passion was always there. She closed her eyes and felt that loving touch.

"Baby," she said.

She reached for the bottle of pills on her dresser and poured its contents into her hand. Thirteen, fourteen, fifteen of the red capsules lay in her palm, like a spreading bacterium.

"False sleep." She dropped the drug and vial into the garbage. "I'd only feel worse in the morning."

CHAPTER TWENTY-THREE

The following afternoon, Marty called.

"Cory's told me what had happened. I'm coming over later. I think we should talk."

A speech, Helen suspected, when Marty's tone had registered disappointment. She was about to hear the age-old "you aren't healthy and your emotions are getting the best of you" speech, or something boringly similar. Whatever.

While she waited, Helen catnapped in her chair. Her night had been long, not with nightmares, but with continual thoughts of Cory and a fight that should never have happened. Anger had replaced logic. Helen had become reactive. Still, she felt betrayed and wondered if Cory's accusations of infidelity were a redirection of her true thoughts. Maybe a smoke screen to hide how she felt about the show.

A heavy pounding on the door startled her awake. "Huh?" she said in a moment's haziness.

"Helen, it's Marty. You okay?"

"Yeah." She steered her chair to the door and opened it. "Some hostess, huh?"

"I was worried something had happened to you." Marty closed the door and then gave Helen a peck on the cheek. "I've brought dinner." She set the bag on Helen's lap and followed her into the kitchen. "We have tomato, onion, and cucumber salad, and fresh salmon. Do you like salmon?" She took the bag from Helen's lap and emptied the contents onto the table. "Just what are you grinning about? You have that peanut farmer look again."

Helen teased. "You said if Chamberlain and I ever—"

"Oh no. You two are already like Gert and Alice B. Hand in hand."

Helen rolled her eyes. "Yeah. Tell me about that one."

"Have you talked to her today?"

"No."

Marty placed the salad into the freezer for a quick chill and searched the oven. "I think, and I say this as a friend, I think you should get your head out of your tush and meet her halfway." She threw her arms into the air in frustration. "Where's the broiling pan?"

"Top shelf, right side. Our goals are different."

"Nobody keeps the broiling pan in the cabinet." Marty gave it a quick rinse. "You should have redefined your goals together."

"She lied."

"Look. I know Cory well enough to understand that she's panicked." She sprinkled the salmon with lemon pepper and chives, shoved it into the broiler, and turned to Helen. She crossed her arms and leaned against the counter. "Coming out is a big damn deal to anyone. There's more con than pro. She's scared, but willing to stay in your relationship if you come out alone."

"Yes, but it doesn't make sense."

"Yes, it does. In her mind, she feels less threatened."

"She's too willing to write me off."

"Come on, Helen. It was tough for her to admit the truth. Besides that, here you sit, writing her off as well." She took two plates from the cabinet and grabbed some silverware. "Even if you have to fight like alley cats first, you can come up with a solution. Scratch each other's eyes out if you have to. It could be worth it."

"I think I'll let her suffer for a while."

"And how will you handle your own suffering?"

She watched Marty shuffle their dinner around the kitchen and considered her words.

So maybe I am suffering a little. A lot. Okay, a lot. We'd spent nearly three months together, day and night or on the phone when she was away. I love her, I miss her, and what the hell am I doing sitting here? I'm pouting. I'm mad. Damn mad. She didn't put up enough fight for me. Bullshit to her. She was an emotional midget. "*Compromise*." That's all she had to say.

"Compromise," Marty said and stressed the word with a meat fork. "I think you owe it to each other."

"When I buy Chamberpot a thesaurus, I'll pick one up for you, too."

Marty shrugged. "It's up to you. My immediate concern is for perfect salmon." She pulled the sizzling steaks from the oven. "These are gonna be great." The phone rang. "Shall I get it?"

"It's okay. I'll be right back." Helen steered herself into the living room and picked up the phone. She didn't have to check caller ID. She knew who was on the other end. "Hello."

"Are you ready to talk to me?"

Only twenty-four hours had passed and already Helen missed Cory's voice with a passion. There it was again: that brain-dead speechlessness Helen had felt with their first telephone conversation. Wishing to be near Cory, who awaited an answer, Helen sighed deeply. "What is it about you, Coryell

Chamberlain?" she finally managed to say. "I can't resist you."

"I think it's my swordtails."

Helen laughed. "I think it's more than that."

"We need to talk."

"I miss you," she admitted. "I'm angry, but I love you, baby. Compromise, huh?"

"Or concede, give and take, a settlement—"

"Okay, smart-ass. Come over tomorrow. We'll talk."

"I love you, too. Good night, Helen."

When Helen entered the kitchen again, Marty set down her glass of Chardonnay and laughed loudly. "Gotcha."

"What?" Helen asked, trying to conceal her smile.

"You're doing that Carter thing again. A compromise, maybe?"

Helen bit her lip and shrugged. "Maybe."

"Yep. Really made her suffer, didn't you?"

Helen felt her dimples go their deepest ever. "Eat your dinner."

❖

As it turned out, Cory's idea of a compromise wasn't much at all. She agreed to live with Helen but wouldn't display their relationship in public, and, of course, she wouldn't do the show. Back to square one.

"I don't like it," Helen said. "You'll be guilty by association. If I'm the subject of gossip, I'd prefer it was legitimate."

"I think the important thing is that we're together." Cory squeezed her hand.

Helen sulked while she glanced over Cory's face. She liked her features. Her slight overbite gave her mouth a very desirable look. Not so much as a freckle marred her complexion, and she wore makeup only for performances. She was almost always fresh and natural.

She fooled with Cory's wispy bangs. She smiled at her eyebrows. They were always ragged and erratic, never to lay normally. They were cute, Helen thought.

She looked down to Cory's hand. The touch she adored. Cory reached to Helen's chin and raised it. She always wanted to see Helen's eyes when they talked. Only in the music room, when she had said no, had Cory not been able to look directly at her.

"If someone asks if we're lovers, will you deny it?" Helen asked.

"I would be denying you. No. I would say the truth."

Helen huffed. "That's what I don't understand!"

"Boston. It's that simple. There's a better chance of me staying with the orchestra if I don't do the concert."

Cory's eyes stole Helen's heart every time she looked at her, as they did at that moment. Helen relented. Cory would have Boston and the girl; Helen would have the show and the girl, but only in the privacy of their own home. Home. They still hadn't settled on the issue of whether or not Helen would move to Boston. There was time. Either way, she agreed to Cory's terms. Society had won.

❖

Helen tried not to, but she took the compromise personally. She moved back in with Cory, but feeling more an embarrassment to her than her lover, Helen picked random fights.

"I'll be home next week to take you to the doctor," Cory said during a practice break. "Have you been getting more feeling in your foot?" Helen continued to polish her nails and nodded yes. "I look forward to walking with you."

Helen looked up from the table. She said nothing and then continued to apply a second coat of polish, as though she'd never heard Cory. Cory grabbed Helen's hand to stop her. Helen pulled away.

"I'm talking to you, not to the fish."

"I don't think you should come to my appointment. I could need support and you may have to touch me in public."

"Oh for God's sake, Helen. Don't do this to me."

"What the hell are you so afraid of?" She stabbed the nailbrush back into the bottle and twisted it closed.

"We've been over all this!" Cory raised the volume of her voice to match Helen's.

"What's the worst thing anyone could do to you?"

"Take away the one passion I've spent my entire life nurturing."

"I'm number two on your list?"

"That's not what I meant."

"What did you mean when you said you would do a show like ours if you had someone to show off to the world? Well, here I am, baby, and all you really want is to show off with your piano and baton. Period." Helen wheeled toward the bedroom. Cory followed, but stopped at the doorway and faced Helen.

"And what makes you so self-righteous? The world won't magically open their arms to us. They don't like what we do."

"Chamberlain, one day you'll wake up and the only thing you'll have is your damn piano."

"Is that a threat?"

"It's the truth, Cory. You're pushing me away."

"You're pulling away. If you can't handle things the way they are—"

"Now look who's threatening."

"I've had it with you." Cory threw her arms out to her sides. "Take me as I am or don't. You've pulled this crap attitude for two weeks and I don't want to hear it anymore."

Helen followed Cory into the bedroom. She wanted to break the Chamberlain emotional barrier. Anger wasn't enough. She wanted to burst into Cory's brain, and then scratch and claw until Cory realized there was more to life than the almighty concerto. There was Helen, who wouldn't play second for want of an orchestra.

For want of an orchestra, the girl was lost.

Cory sobbed and wiped her cheeks of tears. "Do you think this is easy for me? Why can't I make you understand—"

"Marty isn't afraid."

"She's not the issue. Screw her."

Helen didn't think. She blurted, "Maybe I do."

You idiot, the sensible part of Helen said.

If there was ever a moment in her life when she wished she could retract her words, it was then. The sentence was simple, yet volatile enough to hasten the death of any relationship, but it was a lie.

Cory looked up and the disappointment in her eyes nearly killed Helen. "Well, I hope it's as good for her as it was for me." She stormed out of the room.

"What do you mean by 'was'?" Helen yelled down the hall and Cory charged back into the room.

"You won't let me near you anymore." She mimicked Helen. "'It's uncomfortable.' 'I don't feel very feminine.'" Cory shook her head. "Fine. If Marty Jamison makes you feel—"

"I didn't mean it, Cory!"

"Whatever the case, there'll be no damage control. Obviously, I don't make you happy."

Cory left the room. Helen needed to find one of Einstein's wormholes and climb through it, to go back in time. Only two minutes, that's all she wanted, but there was no means of escape. All she had to work with was the present.

"Cory, I'm not sleeping with Marty," she repeated when they met in the kitchen.

"Look. We aren't working out and I'll take the responsibility. Maybe it's best that I'm leaving in the morning."

Helen took a breath and her voice quivered. "This is really happening, isn't it?"

"I can't be what you want. Go back to your apartment. We shouldn't do this to each other any longer."

"I love you."

"You love my image."

"What?" Helen's blood boiled. "*You* love your image. I don't give a rat's ass if you can play—"

"I've worked long and hard for what I have," Cory yelled. "If you can't respect that, then to hell with you."

Helen abruptly leaned forward. "I'd like to slap you, but I can't get out of this frigging chair." She banged its side with her left hand. Cory walked over and knelt beside her.

"Take your best shot."

In a split second, Helen ended their argument with a strong blow to Cory's cheek. Cory never flinched, but heavy tears rolled from her eyes. Deafening quiet surrounded Helen— who sat frozen in her wheelchair. She closed her eyes. When she opened them, it would be a different time. *Not real...a dream...I didn't hit her.* She opened her eyes only to witness red marks where her hand had connected with Cory's cheek.

"Oh, baby." She reached toward the swelling cheek. "I'm...please forgive me. Oh God, Cory. I'm so sorry that happened. Please—"

Cory leaned away from Helen's hand. "We've said enough, Helen." She rose to her feet. "I'll stay with Liz tonight. Please be gone when I return." She walked out of the room, grabbing the suitcases that she packed for her trip.

"What about us?" Helen asked, on the verge of tears.

"It doesn't exist." She opened the door. "Good-bye, Helen." There was no pause, no turning for a final look at Helen. She closed the door, not with a bang, and barely with a whimper.

Helen waited, expecting Cory to walk back in. She looked at the handle and watched for it to turn. Then she fumed. The nerve of Cory to group her with past lovers.

"I don't love your image," she yelled at the door. "I don't need your image, and I certainly don't need your insecurities."

Still she waited, but as quickly as Cory had entered Helen's life, now she was gone. There was never a middle moment for them.

"Good-bye," Helen finally said over the soft gurgle of aquarium bubbles and silent fall of her tears.

It took only a few hours for Stacey to transfer Helen's belongings back to her apartment. Some clothing, her father's war memorabilia, and her computer system. She had planned to wait until she was out of the wheelchair before she moved in with Cory totally. At least waiting had been smart.

❖

Helen read the papers and so kept up with Cory's concert dates. Her reviews were terrible. Cory was labeled a second-rate talent by one critic, while another insinuated that she didn't know a C scale from a fish scale.

Was someone feeding the fish? Helen wondered.

As if that review wasn't bad enough, yet another made a comment that probably stabbed deeply. "...wouldn't recognize Chopin from a dish pan."

Cory ended one performance early, due to illness. Another review mentioned that she had been going through some personal problems.

Eventually, her final concert date was canceled.

Helen called and got her machine. "Are you okay? Please call me if you want to talk." But there was no return call after two days and she worried. What had "due to illness" meant? She called Liz.

"Cory's going through a bad time," Liz told her. "She's visiting a friend in Baltimore, trying to sort out the jumble."

A friend. Elinor. An ex-lover.

"Watch out for flying piano benches, baby. Flying hands," she said to the photo that Stacey had given her.

"Let Cory do what she has to," Carolyn said. "Take your own space and worry about Helen Townsend. Let go of control."

"I'm not trying to control her."

"But you're trying to do things when you should be healing yourself. Think of what you need more than Cory—to get healthy."

"You sound like Teresa."

"We think along the same lines. Don't burden yourself. You love each other. Remember that. And no matter where she is, she's loving you."

❖

Nights were increasingly difficult. The dreams, the screams, a consuming fire, and they always involved Cory leaving her seat and walking into the flames.

"Cory!" Helen yelled and awakened to an empty bed and their black-and-white photo.

She wiped her eyes, struggled to her good leg, and then removed their picture from the wall. She placed it in her closet. "Feel better in there, baby?" Helen went back to bed.

CHAPTER TWENTY-FOUR

Two weeks after Cory left, Helen's confining casts were removed. Her transition from fully involved with Cory to adjusting to single life was difficult, but she immersed her legs and arm into physical therapy and kept otherwise busy with final preparations for their show. Two days before their curtain was scheduled to rise, she saw Teresa for a follow-up appointment.

Helen eased herself from the white, crackly paper of the exam table.

"How do your legs feel when you walk?" Teresa asked, after completing her own examination.

"Heavy. Stubby. I don't know. There's still some nerve damage, but the ortho doctor assured me that most of the feeling would eventually return."

"Do you feel pain?"

"Sometimes, but it's nothing to complain about."

"How's physical therapy going?"

"All right. I'm still shaky with walking, but I'm tired of using crutches for balance. They're killing my arms." She stepped without using the aluminum supports. Left foot first and then the right. *Right*, Helen urged the disobedient leg. *Come on. Now the right.* She tried again and the leg moved forward.

Maybe the crutches were her friend after all. "Sometimes I think my leg's been disconnected from my brain."

"It's been straight as a board for almost two months. The ease and range of motion will come back with therapy. It's just inconvenient at this point. Take some slow steps."

Helen placed her left foot in front of the right and shifted her weight onto Teresa.

"No." Teresa gently pulled herself away. "Hang on to me, but take your weight on the foot unless it hurts."

She took several more steps with greater confidence, but she didn't like the gimpy irregularity present in her gait. "Still better with support. I hope my limp goes away."

"It's unlikely. You're sporting about a half pound of titanium, and the joint won't be perfect, but it'll be useable. I have something that might help." She rummaged through a tall cabinet.

"They forgot to mention that tidbit, or maybe I forgot." She walked gingerly around the small exam room to loosen up. "What are those for?" she asked when Teresa held up two canes. One was black enamel with a brass handle shaped to fit the palm. The other was green. Chamberlain green.

"Lacks glamour, I know, but you'll be more comfortable using one instead of the crutches. You'll get the support you need." Santos smiled. "First one's on me. What'll it be?"

"Black," she said immediately. When handed the cane, she reached for the other. "No, green."

Sucker.

"Take your time. Don't stress your legs. Moderation is important."

"Yeah. Okay."

"Soak in a hot bath when you can. I also want you to try some exercises in addition to what your physical therapist tells you." Teresa reached into a drawer, withdrew a paper, and handed it to Helen. Then she reached into her jacket pocket and pulled out her prescription pad. She wrote quickly and handed the page to Helen. "Here's a few more painkillers, in case you actually don't listen and end up in tears." She smiled. "Now, there's one more matter. Carolyn told me about Cory."

"Whatever happened to patient confidentiality?"

"Physicians in conference. Are you all right?"

"I suppose." Helen shoved the prescription into her handbag. "I'm better about it."

"You know you can call me."

"I know." Helen stepped closer to Teresa. She hugged her, using both arms now. "Thanks for helping get me back together."

"You're a lucky woman."

Lucky? She was alive, yes, but Cory was gone, Blair was dead, and Helen had a bum foot. They left Teresa's office and met Stacey in the waiting room.

"Keep an eye on her, Stacey, and thanks for bringing her over."

"Will do. You look hot with that cane," Stacey said as she helped steady Helen. She pressed the down button when they reached the doors.

"I guess I'm getting closer to walking on my own two feet again." They entered the elevator, and Helen pressed the L button for the lobby. They descended, and she stared at the blazing letter. Lesbian. Lover. Loser. But she had her health, whatever the hell that meant. She laughed without meaning to.

The bell chimed and the elevator doors slid open. They stepped out onto the shiny, over-buffed floor of the professional building. Through giant glass doors, Helen noticed a light snowfall and signs of a wicked wind. Pedestrians huddled into their coat collars, heads down, hiding from the icy blasts of wintry air.

"Wow!" a woman said when she came through the door. A whistle of air followed. "This has got to be the coldest month." The woman groaned a shiver. Helen offered a polite smile but said nothing.

She looked down at her cane. "It's just you and me, kid."

Stacey corrected her. "Many people love you, Helen. Cory isn't the only person with the privilege."

Helen didn't respond but took Stacey's hand into hers. She pushed through the door using the rubber tip of her cane, her staff of Moses, and then Stacey hailed a cab. The show's group was meeting at Marty's at two for a final off-stage rehearsal.

❖

It was after their practice, when they talked until early evening about their show. They'd each carried on the tasks of developing their acts and had settled on a name for the event. Helen agreed with their choice: "The Stars Night Out."

"This show will change our lives forever," Helen said. "We don't know if that will be for better or for worse."

"We'll need to support each other. That's very important," Marty said.

"Family," Jenny said. "Let's not forget our loyalty."

Stacey raised a glass of orange juice. "To family," she said.

The others raised their drinks and answered in unison, "To family."

The men cleared the table, grumbling in their macho way.

"Isn't this why God created women?" Jay said, and Jackie slapped him with a dishtowel.

"Don't invite me to your place," Jenny said. "I can see it now—"

"Mounds of dishes everywhere," Stacey said.

"I have a woman come in," he said.

Kim missed the point and jumped in. "See? A woman! Men do need women."

"Kim," Jackie said, "you've just set women back about fifty years."

Helen took Marty's arm and they walked into the kitchen. The others could have their brawl alone. She was quiet while she rinsed their dishes and Marty loaded the dishwasher.

"How does it feel to have your legs back?" Marty asked, taking two plates from her.

"Tiring. I'd forgotten how much work walking is. I need exercise."

"Well, give me a holler. We can go to your club or get fresh air at the park."

Helen mumbled to herself. "I wonder if Ms. Frosty is still in a heap."

"What's that?" Marty dropped the flatware into the basket. "Let go of it."

"That's what Carolyn said," Helen said.

"She told you to let go of the plate?"

Helen felt a tug on her arm and realized that Marty was wrestling her for the porcelain. "Oh. No." She released the dish. "She said to let go of the guilt." She dried her hands and Marty flipped on the dishwasher.

"Done," Marty said and slapped her hands together.

"Come on. There's something I have to say to the Bickersons in the other room."

Helen gathered her friends in Marty's living room. Marty sat across from her.

"Is this another pep talk?" Jenny asked.

"I think she's going to ask Marty out and wants us here to shame Marty into it," Kim said.

Helen laughed and looked at Marty. "Would I have to shame you into it?"

"No way, sweetheart."

"I'll keep it in mind." Helen looked at the group. "I want to talk about Blair."

"Go ahead, Helen," Mark said.

Helen thought for a moment. She watched while smoke from Marty's cigarette spiraled upward and scattered into different directions. There had been smoke that night.

"Blair touched our lives from many directions, on screen and off. I don't think I've ever met a woman like her." She paused while heads nodded in agreement and smiles invaded her friends' lips. "The first night I met her, I thought she was obnoxious, rude, undisciplined, and a lush. And she was. I think all of you will agree, but that was Blair. She was a pain in everyone's ass, but also warm and intelligent and funny and sensitive. She was a friend."

Marty wiped tears from her cheek and she reached for Mark's hand. Phil stood with Nick, their arms around each other's waist, and stared at the floor. Jenny curled up on a chair and closed her eyes. Jackie came up behind her and rested her hands on her shoulders. Jenny sat quiet. Kim walked to the window as the back of her hand caught a tear. She looked outside and listened while Helen continued.

"And she was always straight with us, whether we liked it or not." Helen smiled at a memory. "She once told me I look like a sad cocker spaniel when I'm not smiling." Her smile vanished and then her emotions broke. "I tried to protect her.

Maybe if I hadn't pushed her downward—" Stacey came up behind her and wrapped her arms around Helen's waist. Helen turned and buried her face in Stacey's shoulder. "She's gone, I'm alive, and I feel so damn guilty."

"No, Helen," Jackie said. "Never feel guilty for your survival."

"We don't hold you responsible," Jenny said when she reached Helen's side. She pushed the dampened hair away from Helen's cheek. "Blair would have said it was meant to happen that way and—"

"—and we shouldn't make ourselves crazy over something that will never be clear," Helen finished. A deep breath helped her continue. "So I'm accepting my life, and if you're listening, Blair, I love you and I'll miss you tremendously."

"Me too, Blair," Marty said into Mark's shoulder.

Kim walked to Helen's side, knelt, and wiped away Helen's tears. "That was nice."

Stacey cleared her throat and brushed a tear away. "So let's call it a night."

God, that felt good. Helen suddenly jumped. "One more thing! I want to make our announcement at the beginning of the show. How do you all feel about that?"

"I say do it and then we can slide into the good stuff." Marty danced a shuffle. "Dazzle them."

"Whatever," Jay said.

"Okay, Helen," Kim said with a new smile.

United in their purpose, they ended their night with hugs and kisses all around.

"The Stanwyck Theater, right, Helen?" Jenny asked.

"Yes, dear. March sixth. Rehearsal in the morning and be backstage by six that night," Helen said. Jenny was a great costume designer, but also a scatterbrain. And young. Twenty-three. Oh, to be twenty-three.

❖

Helen and Marty lounged on the sofa after the gang departed. Tired from a long day, she yawned and stretched her arms. She rested her head on the back of the sofa. Marty leaned back onto the arm of the couch and an overstuffed yellow pillow framed her head and shoulders.

Marty closed her eyes. "It's gonna be a great show."

"If the patrons stay," Helen said.

"That never occurred to me. Do you think they might leave?"

Helen bounced her cane repeatedly on the tip of her toe. "It's a distinct possibility. We won't lose them all. The gays will stay. They'll be saying, 'I knew he was a queen or she was a dyke.'"

"We should have discussed it." Marty sounded concerned for the first time. "I hope I can handle it."

"Don't do a Chamberlain on me. I've had it up to here with that." Helen drew a line across her forehead. "If you want to bail out, fine. All of you can, but I'll be there."

Marty sat up. "This means a lot to you, doesn't it?"

"Everything and nothing." She tossed the cane to the floor. "Not anymore, I guess."

"Explain."

"What's to explain? Marty, I miss Cory so much." Helen cried and Marty held her.

"Call her, sweetheart."

"I've tried. She doesn't return my calls." Helen moved away. "Can I stay with you tonight? I don't want to sleep alone."

"Sure."

❖

Helen moved closer when Marty snuggled against her back. Warm waves of breath relaxed her neck and she smelled a fragrance of Coco Chanel, number unknown. She wasn't Cory, but Marty was comforting. She wondered how she'd slept alone for all those years after Chelsea.

"Are you scared, Helen?"

Helen laughed. "You're the one who should be scared. You're my fantasy woman."

Marty kissed the back of Helen's neck. "I know I'm not the woman you want. I meant, are you afraid of being alone?"

"I've done alone. I'm afraid of never feeling Cory's arms around me again."

❖

Helen dreamed and Cory stepped toward the inferno.

"Cory!"

Finally, her seat belt now released, Helen rushed to her, grabbed her arm, and swung her around. The bouncing, the screaming, and the screeching stopped. The fire backdrafted. Cory looked into Helen's eyes.

"We're safe?" she asked.

Helen pulled her into her arms. "We're safe, baby. We're all right."

CHAPTER TWENTY-FIVE

S how time.
The night was a shelter from Helen's thoughts of Cory. Backstage at the Stanwyck Theater, nervous excitement charged the air. The men, Helen couldn't figure them out. To them, it seemed just another night, as they sat together in their dressing room, discussing the Knicks and the Rangers. But the women were flying. Dresses went on and came off. Jenny forgot a button and a zipper needed mending. Frazzled, Marty was soaked with perspiration, and her hair frizzed to the appearance of an aged dandelion.

Stacey watched the commotion from a sofa, apparently entertained by their nervous energies.

"Sure," Helen said to her, "be amused."

"I'm gonna pop her one," Kim said, sans smile, while she struggled with her panty hose. "These stupid things. Did a man develop these?"

"Good grief, Kim. They stretch," Stacey said. "Just pull them up."

"That's it." Kim jumped on Stacey's lap and pinched her cheeks. "I've had enough of you tonight."

"It got you on my lap." Stacey grinned.

"Pig." Kim jumped down and continued to wrestle with her panty hose.

"Okay, ladies," Helen announced to her clattering collection of feminine folly. "Jackie, are you finished with makeup?"

Jackie added the last touch to Marty. "All set."

"The house is full and I'm shaking like a leaf." Helen stared at Jenny. "Are you all right?"

"I think I'm gonna throw up." Jenny clutched her mouth and headed toward the bathroom with no time to spare.

"I hope that isn't an indication of the way the rest of the night's going to end up." Marty strutted up to each woman and kissed her cheek. "Break a leg, girls."

Helen held up her cane. "Don't say that."

"Three minutes, ladies," their stage manager yelled through the door. "Get to the wing, Helen."

Helen's pulse quickened. "Come with me, Marty." She took Marty's hand and turned to the women. She looked them over. Jenny came out of the bathroom, pale. "This is it. Relax and have fun out there. We can do it."

It seemed a long walk to the wing. Marty was silent. Helen thought about her sonata and wondered if Cory was anywhere near the city.

"Are you ready, Helen?" Paul asked.

"Yes." She peeked from behind the curtain to an auditorium whose size suddenly seemed to equal that of Shea Stadium. "Jesus," she whispered. The lights dimmed. A man's voice boomed throughout the auditorium. Helen flinched.

"Ladies and gentlemen," he paused, "your host for this evening," another pause, "whose hometown is really Brewster—" The audience laughed with his added piece of trivia.

"Who told him that?" Helen whispered hoarsely to Marty, who also laughed.

"New York's favorite columnist, Helen Townsend."

"Luck, sweetheart." Marty kissed her.

Helen took a deep breath and walked on stage to the dais. A burst of thunderous, rolling applause shocked her. She was never on the receiving end of such a welcome, only ever a bearer. There was no wonder left to why celebrities had egos.

Helen couldn't help but smile. She glanced around the now-darkened auditorium and waited for silence.

"Thank you and welcome. This is a special night for the cast and production crew. Our show will benefit children with AIDS, and your full admission charge will be donated." More applause. Now was the tough part. She waited once more for quiet.

"Before we begin, we have an announcement."

She looked toward the wing, where everyone gathered around Marty. Family. Marty gave her a thumbs-up and a nod. Helen looked back to her audience and realized she was talking to darkness.

"Turn up the house lights, please." A moment later, the darkness lightened and faces brightened. "That's better." She scanned the auditorium and continued.

"This show is a statement by all involved. That includes stagehands, lighting, sound, wardrobe, the entire production team. Unanimously we stand before you"—Helen found herself joined by her friends—"all members of the gay community."

There. It was done. Some of Hollywood, Broadway, and all of Helen stood, naked to the world. Helen gripped the dais while her words met with a dead silence. The only prominent sound was the pounding in her ears. Her palms grew sweaty and she hated the quiet. Then someone coughed and another cleared their throat. Helen's eyes followed the sounds. People whispered to those sitting next to them. Jenny reached for Helen's hand, Marty took hold of Jackie's, and a chain reaction went down the line, joining the group. They became one.

It must have been the gays in the audience who reacted first. Whistles, a few yelps from around the audience, applause from a group here and there. Those things offered little relief. A man in the eighth row stood.

"I didn't come here expecting to see a bunch of faggots skipping around."

"Sit down!" a young woman said. "Don't be rude."

"The men involved with the show are gentlemen, sir." Helen grew more confident, having mentally prepared for the worst-case scenario.

"Nothing but a bunch of queers," the same man muttered and headed toward the exit.

"I'm here to see a good show, Helen," the woman with the white scarf, third row, said.

"And we promise you one." She watched while seven more left their seats, some laughing. "We're coming out tonight for community support. For the children who are not understood, for the parents who are not. For your neighbors and for some of you." Helen watched members of the audience whisper and then suddenly a slow, but strengthening applause rang through the auditorium and delivered a feeling of relief to Helen. "I'm scared to death up here."

"You're a gutsy group, Helen," the man with the woman in the white scarf said.

"Thank you. We have a terrific show for you. Marty would say we're going to dazzle you. And we just might."

"Blair," Kim whispered.

"Oh," Helen said into the microphone and blushed when she heard her voice echo. The audience laughed. "The show is dedicated to another member of our community. Blair Whitman." The clapping of hands was loud and long. Blair still commanded an audience.

Helen introduced the first act, Nick and Phil, who had worked up a comedy sketch. Along with Marty, Helen watched them from the wing.

"You were great," Marty said with excitement. "I almost went after that first guy."

"Thanks," she said and checked her appearance in a full-length mirror. She fussed with her sleeves.

She wore a white, form-fitted dress. Sequins dressed the fabric from shoulders to waist, and the skirt was split up the side. The neckline dipped below her throat, where Cory's emerald sparkled. Helen's cane felt more like a complementing prop than a practical necessity. She looked out to the crowd again.

"What do you suppose they're thinking?" Marty said.

"Who cares? They're still here." She peeked into the audience and was satisfied with their obvious enjoyment of the show thus far. Would Cory have found this so threatening?

Kim was on stage next. She received an ovation and an encore. For her second number, she winged it. "Little Brown Jug" became a liberating, three-variation cello piece. Yo-Yo Ma would have been envious, if not mortified.

Next, Helen introduced Marty. Her songs were sentimental pieces that she had trouble getting through without choking up. The first, "On the Wings of Love," had been Blair's favorite. The second, "I've Grown Accustomed to Her Face," she sang in memory of Blair. Behind her, a screen flashed a series of photos of Blair, from her as a baby to her stills from her final film. The tears evoked by her reminiscence would have been sufficient to water a rainforest.

On they played, some of Hollywood's and Broadway's

finest: dancers, a juggler, a ventriloquist, several actors and actresses. Dancers acted, singers danced, and actors tried it all. Not great sometimes, but always at least good, and often comical, they had a swell time and they charmed their audience.

Intermission turned into fifteen minutes of backstage Keystone Cops, and the joint was jumping. Helen hugged the men and danced with the women.

"We did it! We darn well did it. You guys were great," she said.

Jenny returned from the bathroom, pale after a second run-in with nerves. "I'm learning to hate porcelain. Why am I such a wreck?" She looked toward her jubilant comrades for an answer. "I only dressed you."

"Because tomorrow you're going to see our program printed in every paper in town. Your name will be there in big, bold letters," Jackie said and calmly touched up the makeup on Helen's chin. "You're a target now, Jenny. We all are." She held up the mirror for Helen to give a close inspection. "Look okay?"

"Fine, thanks." Helen propped up her leg for some relief. She ached all over from so much standing. "Jenny, was it your girlfriend that talked to Amanda?"

"I don't know. Maybe. She said she would make some people very uncomfortable." She rubbed her stomach. "I'm doing a good enough job at making myself miserable."

Stacey gave her a big sister hug. "You'll be all right," she said. "All of you will."

"You decent?" a man yelled from the hallway.

"Yes!" came their reply.

The door swung open and their stage manager walked in. He handed Helen a note.

"Do you need a doctor?" he asked Jenny.

"No. I'm—" Marty opened the door as Jenny flung herself into the bathroom again.

"Poor kid," Marty said.

Helen opened the paper and read Cory's handwriting. "A fine job and a wonderful show. I love you." If her entire body could audibly weep and drop a tear, this was the time. "She loves me," she said to the note that shook in her trembling hand. "I hit her and she's here, and she loves me. I have to go out on that stage and not scream into the microphone that I love her, too. How do I let her know that I miss her? That I'm sorry for the pain I caused her."

Helen tucked the note into the front of her dress. If that note was the only way she could have Cory on stage with her, then that was how it would be.

❖

For another forty minutes, the troupe paraded their entire range of talents. Finally, the moment was Helen's. The curtain closed behind her while stagehands wheeled a white grand piano into place.

She addressed the audience. "As you can see from your program, I'm the next act." She hadn't planned on how she would move into her part of the show, so she joked. "Do I introduce myself?"

Marty hurried onto the stage. "You'll do no such thing." She turned to the audience. "Ladies and gentlemen, the woman responsible for bringing us together tonight will treat you to a lovely piano solo. Ms. Helen Townsend." Marty clapped as loudly as the audience.

The curtain opened and Helen leaned closer to the microphone. "This is for you, baby."

She walked to the grand piano and placed her cane beside

her. Her jitters now gone, she felt defiantly confident. Hopefully, the music would strike memories for Cory and would answer her note. Helen knew exactly what she was doing when she began to play.

Memories of retiring to Cory's Jacuzzi; of laughs and long telephone calls from whatever city Cory was thrust into; of Rice Krispies and no haircuts; of Boston and no agreement. Memories of love, of making love, and then it was over. The sonata ended.

"That was fun," Helen said once the applause had subsided.

"One more, Helen," someone yelled.

"Oh, no. One-shot deal. Thanks, but I'm glad it's over with."

One by one, the cast and crew came onto the stage as they were introduced. Each name produced a person, each person voiced a declaration, and each declaration received a burst of applause.

"I'm a member of the gay community," Phil said as he walked out with Nick's hand squeezed into his.

Nick had replaced his suit jacket and shirt with a T-shirt that pointed toward Phil. The shirt read, "I'm With Him."

"I'm a lesbian," Marty said. "Woo-hooo! Freedom!"

"There go my ratings," Mark joked.

They went down the line, each proud to be part of the evening's events. They strutted and grinned. Nearly wrecked with nerves, Jenny held on tightly to Marty. Kim smiled, and finally, all the members of the troupe gathered behind Helen, her cane, and her dais.

By rote, Helen delivered a final speech, while her eyes searched for Cory.

"…higher levels of consciousness…raise the collective conscious…" *Where are you, baby?* "…travel home safely."

Before she could blink, before the audience could stand, Helen heard another voice from the auditorium.

"Helen."

There was no mistaking who owned the sound. Goose bumps erupted on every inch of Helen's body. The audience looked around, trying to find the person who spoke. Helen knew the source but not her location. Somewhere in that dark, cavernous room sat a small, fearful woman, a knight out of armor, who allowed courage to destroy her fear.

"Yes?" Helen asked while the house lights became their brightest.

"May I join you on stage?"

Helen saw all heads turn toward the woman on the end of the tenth row, left of center. Eyes that could be judging, changing their minds; eyes that could connect with Boston and change their minds as well.

"Yes," Helen said and looked to Marty. Marty gave an excited, quiet clap.

Cory made her way down the aisle while a stagehand wheeled out a set of steps.

"Cory Chamberlain," someone said.

The auditorium was quiet while Cory ascended the steps one by one. Helen heard only the slow clicking of Cory's shoe heels as she made her way closer.

Cory looked toward the group she had once been a part of and then walked to Helen. She covered the microphone with her hand.

"The sonata was lovely. I'm proud of you."

"Thank you," Helen said weakly, and wanted to cry. How could she have hit Cory and then accept her pride? Helen didn't deserve her. Chamberlain was a solo act. Give her the stage. It's always been hers.

"Ladies and gentlemen," Helen managed to say. "We have

a final guest. Coryell Chamberlain." Helen stepped away from the dais and retreated to the wing as Cory approached the mic. The applause subsided.

"Good evening. Behind me stand my friends. What they did tonight..."

Helen's thoughts responded. *Who did your braid tonight, baby?*

"I met Helen..."

Met me, loved me, left me. I'm sorry I hit you. You're wearing blue again. You know how I love you in blue.

"...let my hair down..."

Cory reached to the back of her head, pulled out two pins, and gracefully shook her hair free to expose a classy new shoulder-length cut. Helen smiled. *You look wonderful, baby. My incredible edible. Just kind of shake it around a little for me.* Cory turned her head toward Helen.

"...and apologize." Cory extended her hand toward the wing. "Will you be with me on stage, Helen?"

Helen couldn't move. She wanted to run to Cory, squeeze her tightly, smother her in kisses and say, "Hell, yeah, I'll join you on stage, or in the Jacuzzi if you'll have me." *In a heartbeat I would, but, baby, someone nailed my feet to the floor.*

"I deserve that," Cory said after silence answered her. She withdrew her hand. "Then I'll say it alone. I love you, Helen."

Helen's eyes widened. *What? She said it! To the entire auditorium, Cory said it.* Tears filled Helen's eyes.

When Cory extended her hand a second time, Helen broke from her suspended animation and joined her. Applause surprised Helen, and when she came close, Cory wouldn't allow her to stop, but instead embraced her with all the power she could conjure from her five-foot-two frame.

"You feel so good." Helen held tightly while the audience still cheered. "I'm sorry, baby."

"I need you," Cory said through the noise. "Please come home with me."

"I will." Helen tightened her hold and felt a fireball of fear subside. "You'll be safe with me."

With Helen in flats and Cory in heels, they stood nearly eye to eye. Cory took the night a step further for everyone. She leaned into Helen's mouth, kissed her long, and showed them all she was not afraid of their future.

Cory giggled when she pulled back. "We're getting a standing ovation. It's the best I've ever had."

"I love you. Let's get outta here," Helen said.

"First let me play."

"What piece will you do?"

Cory smiled. "The pollen haze," she said, and Helen cringed.

Helen stepped up to the microphone. "Our final guest: Cory Chamberlain and Frédéric Chopin's *Military Polonaise*."

Cory played for the group that surrounded the piano. She played the majestic tune for their individual triumph and for their group. From her dais, Helen listened.

She was in love with that tiny woman on the bench. They would work on their problems, scratch each other's eyes out, beginning tomorrow. They had a lifetime ahead of them, whether in Boston, in New York, or in the fertile farmland of Texas. Well, Helen would fight that one. However, for now, she simply basked in the glow of having her knight return from her private battle, scarred, her own dragons slain, to claim her lady. And Helen would surrender, tonight and forever.

Finished with the selection, Cory returned to the dais and walked Helen to the piano. She insisted that Helen sit on the bench next to her.

"I want to play for you."

"I'll be in your way," Helen said.

Cory shook her head. "No. Never again," she said and began the gentle, romantic music familiar to Helen.

It was the Chopin etude, the special piece Cory had never played for anyone, until now.

About the Author

Bobbi Marolt was born in Pennsylvania and upon graduation from high school enlisted in the United States Army, where she specialized in telecommunications. After an honorable discharge and two and a half years in Texas, she ambled into Connecticut "to go to school." That stunt landed her between New York and Connecticut for the next several years, jammed into quality assurance positions in various types of manufacturing. After a brief move to Las Vegas, she again resides in New England. Her interests include films, theater, and classical music.